COMEBACK

Abandoned as a baby, Gail Knight has lived in council homes all her life and never known her parents. At first, her talent for gymnastics is simply an outlet for her energy, but then it enables her to create her own identity and she is hooked! Winning an Olympic gold medal becomes her burning ambition, and sparks off another goal that she's determined to achieve: to find out who her parents were.

Through weeks of gruelling training, Gail devotes herself to both ambitions, doggedly following up clues that suggest she may be descended from an eighteenth-century slave turned prize-fighter called Midnight. After many setbacks, Gail is on the brink of abandoning both projects when two people enter her life and dramatically renew her determination: Tom Bradshaw, a new gymnastics coach, and Milton Pepper, a talented musician from her school.

A sensitive story that reveals the motivation and commitment of a brilliant young gymnast.

Majorie Darke was born in Birmingham but was brought up and educated in Worcester. She attended the Leicester College of Art and the Central School of Art, then worked as a textile designer for some years. She is married to an artist. They have two sons and a daughter, all now grown up, and live in Somerset.

Marjorie Darke

COMEBACK

PENGUIN BOOKS

PENGUIN BOOKS

Published by the Penguin Group
27 Wrights Lane, London W8 5TZ, England
Viking Penguin Inc., 40 West 23rd Street, New York, New York 10010, USA
Penguin Books Australia Ltd, Ringwood, Victoria, Australia
Penguin Books Canada Ltd, 2801 John Street, Markham, Ontario, Canada L3R 1B4
Penguin Books (NZ) Ltd, 182–190 Wairau Road, Auckland 10, New Zealand

Penguin Books Ltd, Registered Offices: Harmondsworth, Middlesex, England

First published by Kestrel Books 1981
Published in Puffin Books 1983
Reprinted in Penguin Books 1988

Made and printed in Great Britain by
Richard Clay Ltd, Bungay, Suffolk
Set in Baskerville

For Barbara and John

ACKNOWLEDGEMENTS

The author wishes to acknowledge with much gratitude the generous help of the following people – John Atkinson; Pauline Prestidge and Jim Prestidge; Barbara Atkinson, Inge Langley, Geoffrey Langley and other staff and members of the Coventry Olympic Gymnastic Club whose patient guidance and expertise in the field of gymnastics have been of immeasurable value; and Glenys Salway for other invaluable information.

1

'Hi...Gail! Gai-yul...hang about!'

On the right side of the open gates – the free world side
– Gail paused. School din was already in her ears even
before the shout. The prospect of all the rest was beginning to close over her head. A long list.

Chalk dust

Sweat stink

Old cabbage

Teachers

Boredom

Questions questions...hovering already.

She hadn't wanted to go in at all; was still struggling
with the astonishment of getting this far. But the shout,
loaded with questions to come, made her wish fervently
that she could be at the top of the drive. She knew who
was shouting, although the familiar voice sounded
strangely different, like everything else. First day of term.
Kids flocking in. The drive winding up the hill, through
banks of grass and trees dividing the sunlight, to the concrete parking space at the top. Bike sheds filling. Everything the same. Everything different.

Reluctantly she turned and saw Heather Stafford
ploughing up the slope of the road. Her freckled face
glowed strawberry from running and the early September
heat.

Chocolate flake on pink blancmange, Gail thought.
Thick bare legs pink too. Sandy hair springing out like
always. Big grin. In one hand a new school bag. Sprauncy
oatmeal canvas and leather affair with tassels hanging

from the strap. She felt a sudden total disgust for her own tatty ex-army haversack, once treasured.

'Dead keen, aren't you?' Heather panted. 'I've been trying to catch up ever since the bus stop. Where've you *been*? There's a rumour going round you had an accident. Run over or something. That true?'

Gail stared. 'Who said so?'

'Cathy Thomas.'

'She's nuts!'

'So it isn't true?'

The strangeness that had been following her around for weeks, now increased. 'Do I look mangled?'

'Can't say you do.'

'Well then!'

Heather examined her with dark seal-brown eyes. Long ago when they first arrived very new and nervous at Broadhayes Comprehensive, Gail had decided those eyes were a big con. Nothing had made her change that opinion. They ought to belong to a dreamy filmstar figure. Someone sad and romantic. Instead, built round those gorgeous melting eyes was this plump creature, full of bounce and chat. Blessed with a giggle like unplugged bathwater, and about as secret and full of Eastern Promise as an underdone sausage!

The giggle wasn't present at the moment, and the seal eyes contained a hint of restraint which Gail didn't miss.

'If you've been okay,' Heather said, changing her grin for a frown, 'why haven't you been to the club?'

Gail shrugged. She'd known the question would come, wanted to side-step, but knew Heather too well to imagine she'd get away with it. The excuse she'd dreamed up seemed thin. On the face of things there was no sensible explanation for abandoning training after six years of constant hard slog. The reasons filed through her mind, limping and creaking...

Jackie Wells, coach and friend, had deserted her. Gym-

2

nastics was much too demanding. She wasn't good enough anyway. Being chained to training every day cut out other things, other people.

All truths. All lies. All codswallop!

She could see Heather waiting and said rather truculently: 'Life isn't just training y'know. There's other things to do. Thought I'd lay off the slog a bit. Have a holiday.'

'The whole summer?' Heather accused. 'Seven weeks! You must've had some spare hours. We went to Skeggy for ten days, but I've trained all the rest of the time.'

The smugness was irritating, though Gail knew it wasn't intentional. She looked down at the crack between the paving slabs under her feet, half pleased, half resentful at this interest. Keeping silent. Hoping to fob her off, but knowing all the time it was useless. Heather was a sticker. It was why she had got as far as she had as a gymnast.

Heather tried another tack: 'Did you have a holiday – away I mean?'

'Yes, why wouldn't I?'

'All right...I was only asking! Just wondered, that's all...*you* know.'

Gail did know and tried not to mind. Unsuccessfully. Why was it that everyone, even people like Heather who should know better, had this delusion that kids in care were weirdies who didn't do any of the things ordinary families did?

She said flatly: 'We went to the seaside. Dymchurch.'

'*All* of you?'

'You make it sound like a trainload of soccer fans. There's only eight.'

'Thought there was nine. Who's missing?'

Gail cursed inside at making this trap for herself. 'Steve.'

'Steve Miller?' Heather shot a knowing look, hitched

3

her bag further up her shoulder making the tassels dance, and closed in. 'Where'd he go...home?'

'Remand home. It isn't quite the same.' Gail opened up the distance between them again, unable to avoid the touch of acid. The taste-for-scandal expression on Heather's face spoiled the sense of friendship. And when she asked: 'Tell us what he did?' eagerly as if she was waiting to be treated to a king-sized ice cream, the gap between them suddenly seemed more than two feet of air.

Gail felt herself shrink, still furious with herself for breaking her rule and allowing too much liking to creep in. She hadn't meant to like him so much, but they both went for the same kind of things – reggae, sport, films – and he could make her laugh till she ached with his zany mimicking and terrible jokes.

'Go on – what happened?' Heather insisted.

Gail snapped the door shut on the memories. 'He nicked from six houses. Him and another kid from outside.' That's all she would say. Nothing about setting fire to a garage or putting a match to the science lab in the school he went to. It struck her that by saying 'outside' she'd made the Council Home they both lived in sound like a prison. In all the years of living in such places she'd never thought of them that way before. She shivered, speeding up, wanting to lose Heather and the uneasy thoughts. Steve was gone. People always went away.

Heather stayed. 'There's a new coach at the club.' She changed the subject diplomatically, keeping pace. 'Mr Bradshaw. Tom. Only everybody calls him Brad. I think he's better than Jackie.' She glanced to see how Gail would take this and was met with a stone-wall expression. 'He makes us *slave*. Makes us go on and on till we get the moves exact.' She rubbed her shoulder, exaggeratedly. 'He never gets tired.'

'What is he – Bionic Man?'

'Could be!' Heather turned the scorn into a joke.

4

'Reckon he takes me for Bionic Woman. My poor shoulders!' She rubbed harder. 'Know the last part of my asymmetric routine?'

Her mind full of other things, Gail nodded because it was easier than asking for reminders, or coping with Heather's insistence.

'We've replanned it already. It's much better. He said what I'd been doing wasn't suited to my physique...'

Gail deliberately tried to close her ears. Having backed out, she didn't want to talk about the club or any new routines, and when Heather dropped her voice to a dramatic bass saying: 'Just wait till he starts on you! Murder it is!' she said tartly:

'No chance!'

She might as well have saved her breath. Heather moved into gear, lost in a need to relate every detail, and didn't seem to understand.

'... tried out a half backward circle into an underswing and then to a swing forward. Haven't done the whole move on the high bar yet. Shall do tonight I hope – you'll see! And he suggested a new approach to...'

Impossible not to listen! Imagination flooded the feel of stretched and willing muscles through Gail's body, challenging her. She knew in bones and nerves the way it would be. All of her working, smooth and oiled. Not exactly thinking with her head only, but with the very blood running through her veins. A sudden yearning to go back unsettled her decision to give up gymnastics forever. All the moans about Jackie she had managed to tidy away, escaped and flew up in her face like a cloud of angry wasps.

She stopped dead, turning with a speed that made them almost collide. A group of juniors close behind parted and trod on each other's feet, juggling to get round. Heather put up an arm to save herself instinctively: 'Hey... what you at? What's up?'

5

'You.'

'Me?'

'Yes you – going on about the club and me being there. Get it straight and then let's forget it. I'm not going back.' As she spoke the words Gail felt the most colossal sense of betrayal. Up till now she had done nothing except absent herself and avoid saying anything to anyone, except to vaguely brush away any casual questions. When Bob Penrose, who ran the gym club, came round to the Home especially to see her, she had ducked out the back way and taken off. Coming back long after he had left. She watched Heather's mouth sag open. It was something to have stunned her into silence. All of ten seconds before she summoned enough breath to say:

'You're never! Go on, I don't believe it. You're too...*good*!' The last word crawled out, landing squarely on Gail's back like a ten ton weight. The sense of betrayal ballooned. Wrapped in the argument, the rest of the world ceased to exist as all the vague shifting feelings which had pushed her this way and that over the summer crystallized into a strong unbearable empty desolation. She wanted to take off. Run. But overtaking her either side, preventing her, were two of the lads from her year whom she rated low on her scale of acceptable human beings.

'Hi, Cadbury! Got any soft centres today?'

She looked with dislike at the puffy spotted face of Craig Priestley who had made the crack, then at his inseparable mate, Gray Wilkins, with his single earring. Fat and thin. Hard cases with cropped hair, narrow trousers and bovver boots.

'We didn't see you down at the Baths once,' Craig went on. 'Where've you been all holiday?'

'Where d'you think?' A stupid answer. She knew that as soon as it escaped and heard the rowdy laughter.

'Up Crackley Woods with your boyfriend?' Craig suggested. 'Before they put him in the Nick I mean.'

6

They were gold medal when it came to latching on to any gossip. Blowing up the smallest nothing into monstrous joke machines. Most days she would have ignored them, but with her feelings so tender couldn't let the jibe slip, and said tightly: 'Shut your mouth!'

'Friendly ain't she? Thought she'd be pining for us after this long time.' Craig nudged Gray who didn't agree or disagree, but looked faintly awkward.

In her state of irritation, Gail scarcely noticed. They bored her. She wished they would go away.

'She's pining,' Craig went on regardless.

Gray said half-heartedly: 'Belt up, Craig,' sliding a sideways look at Gail which she saw. What it revealed shook her.

Craig turned to him in surprise. 'What's eating you?'

'I said belt up.'

'Yes, belt up both of you.' Gail started walking again, elbowing them out of the way. To be fancied by Gray Wilkins was the last thing she wanted. He hadn't said it in words, but she knew.

Craig grabbed her arm. 'Don't get your knickers in a twist, Cadbury.'

Gail felt hounded and wished fervently she'd wagged it. Gone down to the market or the park. Anywhere that was sane. She shook him off: 'Why don't you take a running jump!' and left at a quick trot, knowing there was no other way of stopping the corn when they were in this mood. She was fed up with the lot of them, her own thoughts included. People could be left behind, but it wasn't so easy to get rid of the clinging spider threads of anxiety and unanswered questions which were there all the time and had increased alarmingly over this disturbing summer. She had worked hard to sit on the questions, but everything seemed bent on dragging them inescapably in front of her eyes. It was like having a cassette loop in her head. The same thoughts revolving endlessly.

7

Jackie gone; Steve gone: who am I; Jackie gone; Steve gone; who am I...

Sometimes there was a small alternative blip in the loop – parents gone. She must have parents. Everyone did, but hers might never have existed for all she knew. In sixteen years nobody had claimed her. A real hard fact. The only fact she had. The rest, the dreams, were a myth, full stop.

Her mouth felt dry and her heart hammered as if she had been sprinting hard instead of coasting along between the bodies crawling uphill. She had passed the first blocks of school building – piles of concrete and glass. The grounds cradling them never failed to reach out to her. Even in her present turmoil, their magic was as strong. Old spreading beeches and thick rhododendrons whose bunched springtime flowers of pink and red had matured into webbed leaf fingers of interlocking dark waxy green. All grouped round wide spaces of grass that had once belonged to a large old house, long gone. She saw it afresh with a strange clarity. As if she was returning after years of absence rather than weeks. Beyond the buildings were playing fields and a wood, unseen, where kids went for a smoke, and she hid when she wanted solitude. Would they look alien too?

She pushed past the bushes and knots of dawdling kids, towards Arden House. All the school names had Shakespearean connections – Stratford being only a few kilometres down the road. Crossing the courtyard in front she felt a powerful conviction that she didn't belong – here or anywhere. The feeling frightened her and she made for the concrete steps leading up to the house, anxious for the protection of walls. But Heather, close on her heels, spurted forward, cutting her off.

'You can't just rush away like that and not explain.'

'I did explain.' Gail tried to slide round, but was out-foxed.

'Fat sort of reasons. None at all that made sense.'

'Why the grilling? You go on as if I'm doing something bad. Chickening out or something.'

'Well aren't you? What else would you call it?'

Gail felt hot blood rushing up her neck and into her cheeks.

'Chicken,' Heather repeated, aware that the word had gone home. 'Jackie thought so too, when you didn't turn up those last two weeks of term. She told me.'

It was the final outrage. The jealousy that had made Gail deliberately avoid Jackie once the wedding was announced, was clouded over by a vast sense of injustice. 'She told you I'd lost my nerve? What a rotten lie. If anyone gave up it was her. Going off and marrying an Aussie like that...living out there. *She* was the one to give up. She gave up coaching *me!*' Under her rage a small voice was clamouring that this wasn't very fair, but she ignored it, pushing towards Heather, forcing her to take a step up and back.

'She gave up coaching me too and I'm still training,' Heather pointed out reasonably, but still making a cautious retreat.

'What d'you know about it?'

'I know you don't train any more. Everybody knows that. What d'you expect us to think except you're chickening out?'

'What business is it of anyone except me?'

'None. But you can't stop us thinking...only by proving us wrong.'

'I bloody well will!' Gail saw Heather smile as if she had been trying out a conjuring trick and the right rabbit had popped up. Her eyebrows came together in a thunderous scowl, and later she wondered what she might have done if the house door hadn't swung into Heather's back just at that moment. They were pushed up close, nose to chin, both with hands on hips, and looking up Gail saw a

9

sculptured ebony face crowned by a huge circular bush of neat hair craning round the edge.

'Sorry!' A tall spare figure followed, and the face split into a dazzling grin. 'Hi! Playing bookends?'

'Hi!' Gail said, feeling ridiculous.

Heather also said: 'Hi!' then stared. 'Milton – you're *thin*!' Her eyes threatened to leave her head. 'And the Afro, it's... it's...'

'Different,' Gail said tartly.

Heather looked at her with pity. 'Course it's different. He'd got it short before the holiday.' Her gaze was dragged back.

Gail too, couldn't help staring. The Milton she'd known for the past three years had changed a lot over the summer. He was taller. Looked older – almost a man.

'Know me next time I should think,' Milton said without malice, and went on down the steps.

Gail glanced back over her shoulder just as he did the same, his smile replaced by a cool appraisal of them both. Embarrassed, she turned away and saw Heather, like an overripe Victoria plum, gazing past her with obvious admiration.

With a sudden burst of determination to escape all these underground feelings flowing around and her own in particular, she side-stepped Heather and burrowed into the protective noise of the school house.

10

2

Pat Merton blew a wisp of hair from her nose, rubbed the
perspiration off her forehead with the back of her hand,
then went about collecting used tea mugs and smeared
plates with a cheerful bustle and clatter, stacking them in
neat piles on the tray. It had been a busy twenty-four
hours. Starting with a new arrival – poor little mite. Thin,
scrawny, weeping in fits and starts, sleepwalking. Pat blew
the wisp away again. *Some parents*, she thought fiercely, and
sighed. It was difficult to be philosophical at times like
this morning when poor little Lyn's dad burst in half cut,
cussing and blinding and threatening what he'd do if she
didn't let him take 'his girl' away. The court order hadn't
meant a thing!

'Bloody interfering bitch...' The words walloped her all
over again and she felt the same irritation, not at the
words, but at her own failure to cope. Calling the police
was failure in her book. She gave herself a shake. An early
night was what she needed.

She looked at the solitary figure still sitting at the table.
No fear of meddling parents there. What had Mrs
Bridgeman said? Something about 'a difficult case. Hard
to fathom' and the girl being 'tight as a clam about
her thoughts and feelings'. No mystery in that with her
mum abandoning her as a little kid, and no dad either,
poor mite. Lucky she was so pretty. Well, not exactly
pretty...arresting, and a first-class gymnast into the bar-
gain. Mrs B had been uptight about that too – 'Should be
a way through,' she'd said, 'but the girl won't talk about
that either.' Typical damning summary. But then that

11

Mrs B was a bit of a funny woman altogether. Not hard-hearted exactly, but had blind spots and could be very touchy if she thought anyone was going behind her back. She hit the nail on the head sometimes though. It *was* a puzzle why anyone should want to give up something which they excelled at. No sense in it at all!

Pat paused, propping the tray on a well-padded hip – baffled. The girl was in a dream half the time. Now for instance. Head on hands, elbows amongst the crumbs. And those lovely amber eyes staring at ... A wave of concern washed over her. Ought she to sit down now and have a chat? Give her some time ... but there was the washing up and then that phone call to the office and she simply must have a word with Mrs Gill and straighten up that mistake about the laundry or she'd be giving in her notice. Oh Lord ... *time*! But this brooding wasn't good.

'Gail, dear, I'd be very glad if you'd lend a hand.'

No response. Feeling as if she had come up against a brick wall, Pat tried a question: 'Isn't it your turn for wiping up?'

'What?'

'Wakie wakie ... where are you? She waved a hand in front of Gail's eyes. 'The washing up. Your turn.'

Gail felt as if she was being dragged back from a long distance. A great lethargy had settled on her after the barney with Heather that first grim school morning. She had done nothing since but stare aimlessly through classroom windows, loll about outdoors in the break times, and force herself to and from school in a daze. Heather, exasperated, had given up trying to coerce her back to the gym club, and left her alone. Gail hardly noticed; preoccupied with the division inside herself. Two immense pressures leaned on her competing for importance – the urge to find out who her parents were, and an impossible burning desire to become another Malinova. The first was a stone-wall non-starter, she thought, and the second nothing but a laugh. Except she felt as if she would never laugh again.

'Rise and shine, love,' Pat said, very jolly.

With a heavy sigh, Gail got up. Outside the other kids were playing in the garden. Their shouts and the thud of the ball being bounced, wafted in through the open window. She felt totally alone. As if she was a ghost walking about the world unable to make anyone understand that she was there. A sensation which she seemed to have no power to overcome. Her drifting gaze took in the mouse hair, pug nose, wide mouth of the Housemother. Following the plump contours of breasts and spare tyre of flesh not quite under control beneath the tight sweater. Then on to well-pressed jeans and red painted toenails showing against the open flip-flop sandals like an unsuccessful try at being with-it. Gail rose out of her trough enough to decide that she would have liked Pat Merton better if she hadn't tried to be with-it. Then sank back into indifference.

They finished clearing the table, Pat throwing out chirpy bits of conversation. Gail ignoring them.

In the kitchen, Pat tried another question. 'Had a lousy day at school, dear?'

That special voice level! Gail, recognizing what she thought of as a 'butter-up', kept her back firmly turned and shrugged; shoving at a tower of plates knives spoons. The topmost cutlery fell with a crash into the stainless steel sink.

With great will power, Pat bit back the shout of warning that rose to her lips. She pushed up her sleeves. 'Wash or wipe?'

'I'll wash.' Gail turned on the hot tap and squirted in enough detergent to wash the crockery for a whole canteen. A greasy saucepan followed, then glasses and cutlery, sloshing them together in an aimless way.

Again Pat restrained herself. That last Housemother

13

must have been as much use as a month of wet Sundays. Hadn't she shown the kids any of the proper ways of doing things? The whole house had been a disorganized confusion. Everthing done slapdash.

It had been easier before, Gail was thinking. None of this clear-up-as-you-go-along-neat-and-tidy stuff. Auntie Pat! Catch her using that label. The other kids could do as they pleased. She couldn't stand pretend relationships.

Light from the window glanced rainbows off the foam and she scooped a handful, holding them high. Gazing through. Blowing. Mind floating into a more comfortable blankness along with the freed bubbles.

'Lovely, dear, but if you could give me something to wipe...' Pat began but was cut short by a sharp rap on the front door. She put down the cloth she was holding, blew the wisp of hair from her nose again and flapped across the kitchen into the hall.

Dripping foam, Gail went to look. Heard Pat say: 'Hilary... I *am* glad to see you!' and saw her buttocks wobble as she stepped back to let the person in.

A husky voice said: 'You look all in. Lyn been difficult?'

'Nothing I can't handle. But that father...'

'Say no more! He was in the office lunch time!' A small woman in faded grey cords and a sage cheesecloth shirt came into the hall. Unremarkable except for a waterfall of coppery hair sliding over her shoulders. Gail recognized the social worker who had brought the sleepwalking Lyn the day before. She took a step forward for a better look and was pinned by wide cat-like eyes. A smile equally sharp and shining directed at her like torchlight.

'Hello... Gail isn't it?'

Startled, Gail stared back without replying. The sensation of being visible which she longed for, flickered in and out, bringing with it wary suspicion instead of pleasure.

Pat said: 'You've got a good memory, Hilary,' removing the need for Gail's answer, which immediately made her

14

want to speak and act for herself. The feeling thrust into her so strongly it took her by surprise, demolishing her listlessness. She thought later it was one of those nothing-at-all moments which end up changing everything. But now was only aware of rising resentment, grubby hand-marks on the yellow emulsioned wall and a wry hint of sympathy that came and went so rapidly on the social worker's face, it might never have been there.

'Come on in.' Pat went to her sitting-room door, paused for a moment, hand on knob, and looked back over her shoulder. Perhaps an opportunity to show a bit of initiative might be a good thing? It was worth a try. 'Finish the washing up, Gail, there's a dear. If you are feeling really big-hearted you could make us all a cup of tea couldn't you?' She offered a positive smile and went in, closing the door.

Stuff you and your tea, Gail thought, going back to the kitchen all the same. Doing a record wash dry put-away, so that she could get to the action before her courage ebbed, or somebody barged in and wrecked the plan. Afterwards creeping from the kitchen upstairs. In the bed-room she shared with a girl called Carol and the sleep-walking Lyn, she dragged out her training bag. Pants, socks and tights, jeans, a couple of T-shirts, shoes, money, a skirt – she stuffed them all in. If anyone asked she'd say she was going down to the club. Then hurrying out of her school clothes, she pulled on leotard, track suit and train-ing shoes as a further camouflage, and went down into the street unnoticed.

'Hi!' Milton thumbed at the empty seat beside him. Gail groaned inwardly, but had no choice. The bus, start-ing with a jerk, sent her lurching into it, and in wedging her training bag on the floor under her legs, she acciden-tally knocked the guitar case he was nursing.

'Hey ... watch it!'

15

'Didn't know you played one of them things.' She felt prickly, wishing she'd been allowed to take the ride to town unobserved. There was so much to work out. Running off had been impulse. She had to think it through.

Milton looked surprised. 'Been playing for yonks. Thought you knew.'

'How should I?'

'Everybody knows. Besides we've been in the same year group at school long enough.'

'So what!'

'There ain't much as don't get around in three years.'

Which was true. How *had* this bit of information slipped past her? She gave him a sideways look, on the point of saying she wasn't that interested in what he did, but got side-tracked by the fascinating transformation in his appearance which hooked her every time she saw him. Her imagination bent him over a guitar, fingers plucking the strings. He'd look really something with that Afro haircut. How very long his fingers were. Strong looking, not stringy like the rest of him. A great contrast to herself. She glanced mournfully down seeing the spread of her thighs. God, she must have put on a ton! Fat and unfit. She should never have stuffed like a pig all summer, but the craving had been irresistible. She came out of these depressing thoughts, hearing him talk, but not catching the meaning of what he had said – something about ten p . . .

'Twenty isn't it?' The bus fare was ready in her hand.

He laughed. A great rollicking sound, throwing his head back and slapping his knee. Several people looked round.

Gail felt distinctly embarrassed and muttered: 'Well it is.'

'That's our name, girl. The Group's. For now anyrate. If you want to know why, it was all we could scrape up between us the day we started. Don't blow your mind, but we're working on it.'

She ferreted desperately after what he must have said, coming up with nothing.

Watching her flounder, Milton explained: 'The Group I play with...at the Centre.' And seeing her still blank: 'The Community place. You know — past the Sports Centre. Going that way yourself aren't you?'

'Maybe.' She felt trapped. As if a fine net had been thrown over her which was drawing tight. If she said she wasn't going straight there he'd ask a load more nosy questions. She said rapidly:

'Thought I'd drop in for a while, that's all. To make Heather shut up.'

'Ah!' His grin was knowing. 'She does go on, don't she...wow! Reckon she could talk a Rolls Royce into settling for two star petrol!'

She was amused in spite of herself and laughed.

'Got through to you though,' Milton went on, fishing a packet of chewing gum out of his pocket and offering it. 'Got you to go in the end.'

She took a piece of gum, unwrapping it slowly. Heather could go to hell! People! Either they were trying to push you into doing what they thought right, or if they weren't doing that, were stuffing their noses into business that was none of theirs. Now if it was *answers*, the sort she wanted to have, that would be something else. Chewing, she stared morosely out of the window, seeing a row of terraced houses with dusty pocket-handkerchief front gardens, litter blowing along the pavement, a dog cocking its leg at a dustbin.

'What made you change your mind?' Milton asked.

'Just thought I would.' Gail withdrew her gaze from the outside world and fixed it on him. 'What's this Group of yours then? The Ten P thing...what sort of stuff d'you play? Are you good?' Somebody else could have the questions for a change.

'Reggae. I dunno about good...yet. We will be.'

Her interest perked up along with the ghost of Steve. 'You don't give concerts then. Or do you? Does anyone come and listen when you practise?'

Milton rubbed his ear reflectively, giving these inquiries some thought, and observing him intently, Gail felt her envy grow. Hating nosiness herself, she was prevented from asking what magic diet had thinned him so beautifully.

'Want to come and listen in?' He returned stare for stare, smile gone, his expression alert and inquiring.

She was instantly on guard, unable to say why, but sensing a subtle difference in him. He was getting personal, as if he was trying to sink the conversation to a deeper level. The ghost of Steve, lingering, came back, and she wondered if Milton knew of that relationship. Of its depth and how it still hurt. Stupid! Everything seemed suddenly stupid – herself included. But how would Milton know? School was a hotbed of gossip. What people didn't know they made up. She stayed sullenly silent.

He didn't seem to notice. 'We ain't done any proper gigs yet, but we mean to. Only been together for a few months. There's a Christmas show at the Centre. Maybe we'll cut our teeth on that.' The smile came back, relaxing his expression into the familiar easiness. She got the impression that he was really pleased by her interest, and felt a little ashamed, though still touchy.

'Who else is in the Group? Anyone I know?'

'Shouldn't think so. No one from school. Gaz Halliday, Jackson Forbes, Clive Braddock.' The names meant nothing. 'I'd ask you to come along now and listen if you were at a loose end. But I know you've other plans.'

For a second she thought – He knows! – and sweated. Then realized he was referring to the gym club. She ran her tongue round her lips, wishing she didn't always jump to the worst conclusion, or feel so pursued. It had happened even with Steve. Like the time he'd asked inno-

18

cently: 'D'you like being given birthday presents?' and she'd flown off the handle, thinking it a dig at her not having parents. All he had been doing was taking care not to offend her! Later she'd discovered he'd eaten the birthday chocolates himself. What a relief not to give a damn about other people's thoughts, but she never could. Hurriedly she asked about the band.

'Oh...a second guitar. Drums. Keyboard. Percussion – Jackson's got a great scene going there. The things he dreams up! Came with this old washboard his gran chucked out. Had a sounding box on the back and all wired up for amplifying. For reggae...crazy!' Milton laughed in the same free way. Rocking the seat. Oblivious of the interest he caused.

He doesn't give a monkey's for anyone, Gail thought, shrinking in her seat. Heather thought he was a real laugh. More like being in the company of a performing seal in her opinion.

They walked downhill past the glitter of a Wimpy bar, glowing shop windows, bus shelters sprayed with messages like 'Boot Boys rule okay' and 'Anyone who wants a kiss be here tonight at six', to the road junction where she should have said: 'T'ra then,' and marched on, but didn't. The last threads of inertia coupled with a secret stubborn resistance to letting him suspect she was going anywhere but to the gym club, kept her walking beside him.

Milton paused at the bottom of the steps in front of the Sports Centre – a huge rising wall of glass. 'Come down after why don't you? We usually go on till half nine or later.'

'I might. Depends.' She didn't want to commit herself.

'Okay. See you maybe.' He raised the guitar case in mock salute.

She was relieved he hadn't insisted, and watched him lope across the road into the car park. An easy relaxed walk like his personality. Then he vanished under the flyover ring-road, and she turned, meaning to go back the way she had come, but was thwarted again. Running towards her was a track-suited figure, Welsh black hair sprouting in elastic-banded bunches either side a letter-box smile that almost cracked the round face in two halves.

'I told Heather she was talking out of the back of her neck. I knew you'd be back,' Cathy Thomas panted.

The instant frustration and anger petered out. Guilty relief took over. Gail took the gum out of her mouth, rolled it into a ball and flicked it into the litter bin. 'Dunno how you could be so sure.'

Cathy wagged her head sagely. 'Know you, that's how!'

Not believing her, Gail said: 'That's more than I do,' and went inside.

3

Gail pulled open the door into the gym and the sounds of activity swelled suddenly as if the volume knob of a radio had been given a sharp twist. Mrs Capucelli, who took the money, sold gym gear, mopped tears and provided a listening ear for all troubles, was sitting at a trestle table. She looked up from the open register. Light from the overhead strip made blind circles of her glasses but Gail could see she was surprised. Then the broad cheeks creased up.

'Hel*lo* stranger!'

Gail tossed back a smile, sidling in, not wanting to be buttonholed before savouring the well-remembered place. The long gym stretched out as familiar as her own body. A place stuffed with memories of agony and joy. She let her gaze wander over the high wooden walls, floor spread with blue matting, apparatus. The asymmetric bars, always her favourite, were at an angle from where she stood. Three girls were humping a mattress into position underneath and she singled out Heather, back turned. Nearer were beams of assorted height; one in finger-touching distance. Beyond them the two-handled pommel horse and parallel bars. She tried to search out Bob Penrose, knowing that she would have to speak to him. Denise, one of the trainee coaches, was chatting to Mrs Lobeck the dance instructor – a spry oldie with dyed black hair and backside spreading and bulging under her ballet tights like a badly stuffed cushion. Kids galore were limbering up, a few boys amongst the girls. Heather straightened herself, caught sight of Gail and flapped her hand

21

like a demented yo-yo. She acknowledged with a nod, still scanning the gym – and saw the broad back of a man in the uniform track suit of navy blue with green striped trim. He was squatting by the vaulting box adjusting the springboard.

He stood up.

She had a rotating view of cropped wiry grey hair, low forehead jutting over deep-set eyes, broken nose and square aggressive jaw. As he came full face, she saw the scar seam carving his left cheek and new immediately that this must be Brad. Knew also about the scar. Heather had mentioned it casually. A description about as punchy as weak tea, Gail thought, staring at the Frankenstein scar. Eyebrow, eyelid and mouth corner pulled into a dramatic downward droop, giving the peculiar impression of two separate moods. She was reminded vividly of masks she had once helped make for a school play. Comedy and Tragedy. She was gawping and knew it, but couldn't pull her eyes away. As if he felt this scrutiny, Brad looked up and directly at her. A glance so penetrating she felt as if she had been sliced through by a laser beam.

He beckoned.

Very reluctantly she skirted the beams, going towards him.

'So you've decided to come back, Gail Knight.' His voice was abrasive, the words squeezing out from one side of his mouth with a strong Yorkshire accent. 'I've been expecting you.'

She was taken aback, anticipating questions not statements, and didn't know what to say. The way his face moved as he spoke fascinated her; damaged side working in a series of little ticks, which went on after he had finished speaking. The scar wasn't just a single line after all, she noticed. A finer scar line wriggled from it downhill. Near his ear was a patch of yellowish skin, evidently put there by plastic surgery.

He regarded her silently for a few seconds, then added: 'Mr Penrose isn't here. He's taken the little Swati lass down to Casualty. Don't know how long before he gets back. You wanted to see him of course.'

'Yes.'

'Hmm!' looking at her with an unblinking lizard stare until she was so uncomfortable she was ready to turn and bolt. But she wouldn't let herself. Nobody was going to get the chance to say she was scared or spineless. She'd had enough of that already. She forced herself to meet his gaze, until from the corner of her eye she saw Heather homing in, looking smug. Some of her bewilderment evaporated. Of course it could only have been Heather rashly spreading rumours about Gail Knight coming back! She really was hopeless. Much too pushy. But it was impossible to be angry with an enthusiastic puppy, all floppy gambolling paws and good intentions! Exasperation, liking and a sort of comic despair ravelled inside. Her heart's in the right place, Gail thought, but what a pair of outsize feet when she gets organizing!

'This is Gail, Mr Bradshaw.' Heather beamed at them both, blithely unaware that the introduction was out of date.

Gail cringed. Brad grunted dourly. Heather's smile faltered a little, but she didn't budge.

Around them the gym was filling up. The electric wall clock registered after five-thirty, which meant that the session was late in starting.

'You intend staying, or is this just a fleeting visit?' Brad asked, forestalling her. There was a dry edge to his voice which made her bristle, but with Heather listening she daren't snap out: 'Staying of course!' She wasn't ready for that sort of decision to be blabbed to the world.

'That's for Mr Penrose to say.'

'You'll likely have a long wait.'

'I don't mind.'

23

'And waste your time.'

'I don't mind,' she repeated, knowing with a sudden cold sinking that she did.

'She could do the warm-up with us, couldn't she? It wouldn't matter,' Heather asked eagerly.

'No harm, but time-wasting like I said.'

'Oh she won't mind that.'

'You reckon?' The dry edge again.

'Oh, no! It's Friday. There's all weekend to do homework. Nearly all,' Heather corrected herself.

Gail felt her hackles rise. They were talking about her as if she weren't there. Bringing back the invisible feeling. Putting a glass wall between her and the world.

'It's my time you're talking about. If I want to waste it I will,' she said crisply, and saw Brad's mouth compress on the good side. Whether to hold back a smile or check annoyance, she couldn't be sure. The doubt he had sown about her being allowed to stay or not, chilled her. It was something she hadn't bothered to consider.

He said: 'A ten-week lay-off is a hell of a time. Jog first. Six times round the gym and barefoot. But keep your track suit on till you're thoroughly warm. Then join the others for the remainder of the usual warm-up.' He turned away, calling for the class to assemble in rows.

It was a temporary concession. A small triumph.

Heather gave her a nudge, whispering: 'Didn't I say he's demon?'

'You didn't say he knew all about me or that he looked like a gargoyle.'

'Half. The other side's okay.'

They exchanged glances and spluttered sudden giggles that they tried to bottle.

'That means you too, Heather Stafford.' Brad's penetrating voice sent Heather scuttling red-faced, to join the end of the nearest row.

Gail dumped her training bag, stripped the shoes and

24

socks from her feet then set off round the gym. As lap followed lap her mild triumph dissolved with the mental pinpricks about her cancelled plan. She was painfully unfit. A condition which grew patently clearer as she joined in the warm-up exercises. Her joints creaked and cried like a heap of rusting metal hinges; limbs heavy as dollops of Christmas pud. She groaned inside.

'Suffering are you?' Brad asked as he leaned one knee in the small of her back, pressing her trunk gently but inexorably forward between her outspread legs. 'A bit of pain never did anyone harm. It's good for the soul. Part of the trade.'

He's *enjoying* it, she thought indignantly, seeing Heather legs spread-eagled, body flat between, easy as a clam on the sea bed. Heather who had puffed and struggled over this split position in the past, while she had found it easy. It was humiliating. She found herself almost wishing for Penrose to arrive. At least that would be a breather.

'A demon and a slave driver,' Heather confirmed when they were working in pairs. 'You first.'

They were supporting each other turn by turn. Handstand over into elegant arched bridge with legs and arms as struts, body curved high.

'Sadist more like,' Gail gasped, collapsing.

'A demon slave-driving sadist,' Heather agreed aimiably. 'Gets results though.' She flipped over and came down into the bridge position with an assurance that was particularly impressive from such a thick body.

Gail, stiff and bruised, was impressed. 'He's much worse than old Penrose. Is he always such a driver?'

'You should be here when he's really keen!'

And that makes two, Gail thought. But their keennesses were vitally different. Brad's would be the relentless tyrannical sort. Did she really want to cope with that?

'Why did you turn up tonight, Gail?' Heather asked curiously.

25

By mistake, was on the tip of Gail's tongue. She turned it into: 'Just fancied seeing the look on your face.'

Heather laughed. 'Pull the other one!' then more seriously: 'I really do want to know.'

So do I, Gail thought. Coming to the gym had only been half a mistake. There was something else. Something mysterious which pulled like a magnet. A sharp memory of the heartaches, failures, pain, grinding slog, taunted her. Could she face all that again? And for what? The rare moment of joy when the movement went right? An even rarer win in competition? But the urge to win, to be best...Yes – oh yes! The sun sparkle of a gold medal and all it stood for, shone suddenly in her head. With it came all the old fierce yearning. A bronze once, but never a sniff of gold. One near miss with a silver by half a mark. But that was a year ago when she was on top form. Now she was fat as a pig. Had never been so unfit.

Gloom descended. A mood which didn't improve when Brad refused to let her divide with the others for apparatus work.

'You're as stiff as an old boot. Need suppling – legs first. Over here.'

He was right of course. No point in chancing injury by trying movements her body wasn't ready to do. But knowing didn't make it much easier.

'Get that left leg up.' He lifted her ankle and propped it on the ledge running the length of the gym. 'That's it. Now lie forward...harder...*harder*...' hand flat between her shoulders; pressing.

The tendons between her legs ached. Her back was tired and unresponsive. She gritted her teeth, refusing to complain. Just this once if never again, nobody was going to have the chance to think she couldn't take it.

'Now the other leg.' He adjusted the line of her shoulders as she closed the gap with her body, drawing up her arms to curve like wings round her head. When the effort was almost unbearable, he said: 'Relax,' and took her wrist, feeling for her pulse and timing it while she stood with her muscles trembling from expended effort.

At the beam Cathy was waiting for Heather to finish her exercise. Waiting, but watching *her*, Gail realized as she sneaked a quick look round the gym. Denise too. And Mrs Capucelli. Why all the interest? Was her reappearance such a mind bender?

The swing door opened as she was trying to decide, and Bob Penrose came in. He stopped for a moment to speak to Mrs Capucelli, waving his long narrow hands to stress what he was saying. Everything about him was thin and overgrown, Gail thought, seeing his hands and feet protruding from his track suit in a way that made it seem a size too small. His thick unruly hair, sun-bleached now, was different. Friendly hair, she'd always considered. But there was nothing friendly about his expression as he turned round and caught sight of her. His thin mouth grew thinner.

'Not bad taking all in all.' Brad let go of her wrist. 'Pulse a bit high, but then you look as if you've been on a diet of cream buns and gobstoppers. We'll have to put that right, lass. Starve thee. That's about the sum of it.' His face twitched into what might have been a smile. 'Reckon you'll manage?'

Gail didn't answer. Scarcely took in the friendliness or the assumption that she was back for serious training. Butterflies in her stomach were starting up a gymnastic routine all their own which grew more frenzied as Bob Penrose walked towards them.

'Well?' Brad looked at her for an answer, then beyond her to Penrose. An expression she couldn't interpret flickered the muscles of his face. Or it might just have been the working of damaged nerve ends. She sensed a strong undercurrent of tension.

27

'What's all this?' Bob Penrose came to a halt beside them, giving her a long cool look.

Gail was nervously silent. He could see she was training couldn't he? What else was there to say?

'I got her to warm-up while she waited for you to come back,' Brad explained.

'*You* did?'

'There's never any point in wasting time.'

'Something for you to think over...and digest,' Bob Penrose said to Gail with enough frost to lower the temperature in the gym by several degrees. 'I suppose you think it all right just to turn up as if nothing has happened. Pick up the threads without explanations?' His thick sun-bleached eyebrows met in a scowling line across his tanned face. He looked very annoyed.

She knew he was thinking of the time he had come to see her and she had run into the garden, vaulting the fence rather than face him.

'Hardly fair,' Brad said mildly. 'It was my suggestion after all and...'

'And *my* suggestion,' Penrose interrupted, crisp and tight, 'is that she collects her gear and goes home.' He speared Gail with a look. 'Where's your stuff?'

A hard knot of anger tightened in the region of Gail's stomach. She knew there was no hope of staying now. She felt bitter and resentful. If he had told her off, only let her come back on certain conditions, even insisted on some kind of punishment, she would have accepted it as fair. But not to listen at all! The knot rose to her throat. Mutely she pointed to the heap flopped by the trestle table.

'Right. Get going...and don't bother coming again.' Penrose made as if to turn his back, but Brad put out a restraining hand.

'Wait on. The lass hasn't had a chance.'

Penrose snorted, shaking his arm as if to get rid of a

troublesome fly. 'Don't make me laugh. She's had more chances than I've had hot dinners.'

'I doubt it,' Brad said, keeping hold. 'But that's by the way. Let her explain now. She did brave it and come. You owe her for that.'

'I don't owe her anything,' Penrose retorted acidly. 'She's already proved herself unreliable. No discipline. There isn't any room in this club for people without discipline. Isn't any room in *gymnastics* for people without discipline.'

There was a fractional hesitation before Brad said: 'Sometimes there can be a good reason.'

'Reason!' Penrose made a spluttering sound – mixture of scorn, disbelief and chilly laughter.

'Aye. It's as well to *listen*.'

'Good God!'

Wedged, unable to escape, Gail felt like a tennis ball being batted between them. She wanted to yell out: 'It's me you're gabbing about. ME. I'm HERE! All that about no discipline isn't true. I never missed a day, not in six years . . . except for German measles!' but her throat was jammed and her voice wouldn't act. Too many people were goggling.

Brad put a large hand on Gail's shoulder, linking her with Penrose. 'Go on, lass.'

Penrose's icy artificial calm cracked, erupting into sudden towering inexplicable rage. 'Are you telling me how to run this club?' Ineffectually he tried to brush away the hand link, glaring down at Gail as if she was responsible for his outburst. He said loudly: 'You heard me . . . push off!'

Gail was vaguely aware of thinking his fury too great to be explained by her presence. She wasn't that important. And she couldn't go. Shoulder in a vice, she was being clamped to the floor. Over the top of her head, Brad roared:

'A chance, man. For God's sake she deserves that!'

And Penrose: 'She's had all her chances round here. Take your bloody hands OFF...'

The explosion reverberated round the silent gym. In an agony of embarrassment and misery Gail found extra strength. She wrenched from the restraining hand. Ducked. Wriggled. And was free! Shutting her ears, channelling her vision so all she could see was her training gear, she rushed to it, grabbed and burst from the gym. In one continuous run she took the girdered bridge, snack bar and stairs to the foyer, stopping only on reaching the creeping greenery and notice boards that made part-time walls beside the swing doors. She was still barefoot. In leotard and nothing else! Hastily she pulled on her track suit, socks, training shoes. All fingers and thumbs tying the laces. An ocean of tears wallowed inside. Bobbing on top, Brad's plea to give her a chance. All down her life chances had never been there, or had been taken away. Well, that was over. She'd force the chances. Do what she'd intended in the first place. Get a railway ticket and go.

Pushing through the heavy glass doors, she went down the steps and across the courtyard with her back firmly turned on the Sports Centre.

It wasn't until she had walked the length of the street that the thought occurred – go where? Hot on its heels came a second thought. Why in blazes had Brad, a stranger, stood up for her? She could think of answers to neither.

4

'I'm sure you all remember clearly me explaining last lesson that we shall be studying the British Empire and Commonwealth from the middle of the eighteenth century to the present day.' Jimmy Lomas looked at Five A sardonically, and ran a fingernail between his two protruding front teeth to ferret out a piece of apple lodged there. He was fond of apples. An apple a day kept the doctor away...but possibly not the dentist. The apple chip remained firmly wedged.

'Political and economic structures,' he went on, observing that the girl sitting by the window was staring down into the courtyard below with a glazed faraway look in her eyes, apparently not listening to a blind word he was saying. Strange eyes. He'd noticed them before. Amber. Reminded him of a cat he'd had as a lad. Aloof little beggars, both of them. She had that blank cat-like stare too. As if she was sizing you up and finding you wanting. Disconcerting.

He resettled his suede jacket and smoothed back a fallen strand of sparse hair. 'The slave trade played a large part in this. Several ports grew very fat. Bristol, Liverpool, London. But the effect on the world as a whole was far-reaching.' The apple chip finally gave in and he flicked it towards the wastepaper basket. Missing. Somebody sniggered. He frowned. 'You won't be expected to answer direct questions on slavery in your 0-level exam, but we shall spend a certain time studying the trade in order to understand whether, by significantly increasing personal wealth, it helped to bolster England's economy.'

Not a blind word was she taking in!

'So perhaps you'd like to tell us which cities grew fat and on what, Gail Knight?'

Hearing her name but nothing else, Gail pulled her gaze from the window, almost grateful for the interruption. Below, a curious little scene, like a silent movie, had taken place. Brad had appeared round the corner of the Arts Block wheeling an ancient green bicycle. Almost simultaneously, Mrs Price, one of the PE staff, small and bouncing in a blue track suit, came from the opposite corner by the gym with that trendy social worker, Hilary whatsit. They met halfway. Brad spoke. The women stopped. There followed a conversation which used hand gestures, head nodding and some smiles, but none from Brad. Finally Mrs Price pointed towards the Administration Block. Brad shook his head, turned his bicycle round and all three plus bike disappeared behind the tall beech hedge shrouding the car park.

This unexpected appearance linked in with the endless skein of thoughts which had been winding round in Gail's brain all day. Acutely embarrassing thoughts about herself weakly letting Milton divert her into going to the Sports Centre; herself being bawled out by old Penrose; herself the reluctant patsy in that near punch up between him and Brad; herself and the crazy decision to run off which had died when she'd reckoned up the money stakes, the Castle in the air reverting to the Home on the estate.

'Why didn't you tell me before, instead of leaving it till you get back?' Pat had demanded, dropping into the armchair by the electric fire in her sitting room and indicating to Gail she should sit opposite.

'Nothing to tell.' Gail had perched on the edge, avoiding her eyes, angry and humiliated.

'Don't talk daft! I'm talking about saying where you were going. You aren't a little kid. You understand perfectly well I have to know where everyone is while I'm on duty...' she had paused, taking a deep breath, 'and even if I wasn't, I would want to know you were safe... I *care*!'

The change of tone, the unexpected statement, had shaken Gail. Inadvertantly she had looked up, met Pat's eyes and seen a spark of pity. The moment of warmth vanished. Pity! She didn't want that from *anyone*.

She had stood up, saying woodenly: 'Can I go to bed now?' refusing to listen, to look, to let there be any further communication.

Upstairs, Lyn was already in bed and Carol was coming back from the bathroom. They had pounced on her, bombarding her with questions.

'Where did you go... what happened... was she mad at you...'

All she would say was: 'I went down to the club,' getting undressed swiftly, climbing into bed, turning her back on them both and burying her face in the pillow.

'We're waiting, Gail.'

For the second time Gail dropped out of her thoughts back into the present and the classroom. Sniggers of suppressed laughter greeted her. What in hell had he asked? She looked desperately for help and saw Milton point at his own face, then slit his throat from ear to ear with a finger.

'Assassination?' she tried hesitantly.

Laughter bellowed out. Jimmy Lomas raised exasperated eyes towards the ceiling. Gail glared in anger.

'All right... all right. Joke over!' Jimmy Lomas clapped for silence. 'We were talking about the slave trade, Gail. You'll have to catch up as part of your homework. I'm not going over it all again. Anyone who can't be bothered to listen will only have themselves to blame when exam day arrives and there's nothing in the old brain box but empty space.' She was doing it now – that blank cat-like stare. Looking at him as if *he* was in the wrong! Cheeky little piece. She'd flowered astonishingly over the summer. An underdeveloped shrimp before the holiday and now look at her...leggy; busty! Several of the lads had given her a second look. She'd have to get rid of that freezing stare before she was much older though, or she'd ruin her chances. Most kids would have gone scarlet at the broadside he'd just fired. Not that it was easy to tell with that bronzy skin. But she wasn't showing any sign of discomfort. Obviously loved herself. Probably had doting parents and ruled the roost at home.

He reorganized two Biros, a pencil and four paper clips on the table in front of him. 'Just one more point before we move on. Bristol Museum is putting on an exhibition about the slave trade in a couple of weeks and I shall be arranging a coach trip to see that and Brunel's ship the *Great Britain*. The cost will be about two pound fifty, but I'll be able to give you exact amounts with all the other details at a meeting in room eight after school tomorrow. There will of course be a letter to take to your parents. Try and come if you possibly can. It's very important to understand the background to this section of your syllabus. The exhibition should be very revealing.'

There was renewed laughter. Someone whistled. He thought – God, why don't I watch my tongue! Then smiled knowingly. 'Ten out of ten for quick reactions...just testing! Don't forget to come to the meeting *tomorrow*. Oh...and don't forget to warn your parents *tonight*.'

5

'Slave collar of course,' Milton said as they came out of the classroom and clattered down the staircase into the muggy afternoon sunlight of the courtyard. He imitated what Gail had taken to be a throat-slashing mime.

'How did you expect me to guess that when I've never heard of them?' she demanded.

'Girl, you're a thickie!' Milton cooled his words with a friendly grin. 'Fancy not knowing one of the facts of life.'

'Oh stuff! *I* didn't know either, so that makes two of us,' Heather said.

Gail felt a lift of pleasure.

Milton pulled a face of comic despair. 'Both rubbed out!'

Even as a joke, Gail wasn't going to take this. 'All right then, how come you're so well informed and we're not?'

'Guess you go around with your eyes closed and your ears buttoned,' he said solemnly.

'Oh ah...and I suppose you don't?'

'No.' He hitched his bag to a more comfortable position and began whistling through the space between his otherwise perfect front teeth.

'Come on then...how *did* you find out?' Gail insisted.

Milton relented. 'This old dear who lives near us told me. I suppose it was a bit far-out, but it was all I could think of on the spur of the moment. Not that it did much !' He let out a shout of laughter.

'Oh yes, and how does she know?'

'Because her brother married this girl whose great-great-great...I dunno how many greats...grandad was a

35

slave. I've heard her telling me Mum. She's always in and out of our house. Second home, she says. Her and Mum get on great.'

'Fancy knowing someone who really had a relation who was a slave,' Heather said wonderingly, eyes fixed on his face.

Milton frowned. 'Not all that mind-blowing. It's quite ordinary really. Depends where you come from.'

'Where did the sister-in-law come from?' Gail asked quickly to help Heather out.

Amusement sparkled in Milton's eyes. 'London,' he said and burst out laughing all over again.

Gail couldn't help joining in. When Milton laughed, everyone laughed whether or not they knew the joke. Even Heather was giggling.

When the laughter had died down, Gail said: 'She couldn't have come from London always. She must have come from overseas originally.'

'No she didn't, the Great-Great did that. *She* wasn't an immigrant, she was as English as they come.'

This seemed perfectly logical to Gail when she thought about it. She wondered why she hadn't worked it out for herself. Lots of kids had West Indian parents, Chinese parents, Indian parents, Irish parents, but were born, had grown up here and were English. Or no parents, she thought. And what did that make her? She heard Heather asking:

'Did the Great-Great wear it till the end of his days?'

'Nope. Took it off when he got to England and was freed. And don't ask me what he did with it. All I know is that some bird or other helped him cut it off. If you want to know any more you'll have to come and ask this old dear yourself. She wouldn't mind. Yatters on all day if you encourage her.'

'She sounds a bore,' Gail said.

'No she ain't. She's quite interesting really if you've got

a week to spare. Done all sorts. She went out to France in the First World War nursing and nearly got rubbed out when a shell landed on the hospital. After, she went to Canada. Then there's all these relations – a whole mass – parents, brothers, in-laws. But now there's none of 'em left, only her and her moggie. Guess that's why she comes round so much.' Milton grinned. 'Know what she calls that mog?'

'No. What?'

'Helen. Says she can get rid of all her spleen shouting 'Hell' down the back garden every night!'

They all laughed and Gail asked: 'What's her name?'

'Mrs Box.'

They crossed the path where the mown grass ran down to the drive, and the beech hedge ended at the entrance to the car park. No Hilary and no Brad either, Gail noticed, wondering vaguely about both of them coming to the school, then more particularly why *he* had come. The dim hope that it might be in search of her was blotted out. Probably looking for one of the teachers. He might even be a teacher. Nobody seemed to know anything definite about him. Just rumours. The thought was slightly disturbing. She pulled herself up – what did it matter?

Cutting through the rhododendron bushes they took the small gravel path round to Arden House. School was over for the day, and when Gail had stowed some books in her locker there was nothing to keep her from leaving, but she dawdled. Heather, dropped on by Mr Talbot the House-master, had reluctantly gone to take a message to the office.

'You coming?' Milton asked.

Gail shook her head. There was nothing to go for. Nothing to stay for. Just nothing. She felt low and useless.

Milton hesitated. 'Gail...' and hesitated again, his usual easy-going expression changed. He put out his hand and touched her arm lightly; briefly. But it was long enough for Gray, coming in at that point with Craig close behind, to take in the scene. Tucking an invisible violin under his chin, he began sawing away, eyes half closed, whistling 'Hearts and Flowers' with swoops and sentimental trills.

'Drop off skinhead,' Milton said.

Gray abandoned his violin. 'Shut your face, golliwog. Go hang in a tree!'

Gail felt shocked by the viciousness in his voice. She watched Gray scratch his ribs with both hands, grunting and hopping about in pantomime mockery of a chimp. Milton's face went blank as a wall. He turned his back. Several more people had wandered into the cloakroom now. Some of them looked at Gray as if he was mildly insane. Nobody laughed except Craig who was wheezing up against the coat pegs.

Somebody asked: 'What's up with him?'

'Oh *him*!' Gail picked up her haversack and slung it over her shoulder, suddenly loathing the performance. 'Didn't you know, the zoo's only just down the road. He's escaped. The men in white overalls'll be along to take him back soon.' She left the cloakroom, going to the common-room window. When Milton followed, she said:

'Don't they make you sick!' And when he didn't answer: 'Don't you mind?'

He shrugged. 'Not as much as they'd like. I don't take no notice. That Gray's just making himself look a nutcase.' A laugh burst out of him. 'He isn't even much cop at monkey imitations.'

Gail was astonished, but had to smile with him.

'That's better,' he said. 'You've been going about all day looking like the end of the world was round the corner. Is it?'

'Was that what you were going to ask me before?'

His big smile took on a slight wariness. 'Bit more personal.'

38

'Like what?'

'Just wondered what was biting you that's all. Wondered if it was family bother. Not being nosy y'understand? But I know you don't live at home and I thought something might've...might be...' he was floundering. 'I mean, if you wanted somebody to lend a hand...or an ear...'

A tendril of dismay curled round Gail's spine. She was deeply shocked by the way he had crash-landed on one of her most sensitive secrets, and her first reaction was that he was getting at her. But looking at his open anxious expression, she knew this wasn't true. She still felt like giving him the big freeze, but couldn't. The offer had been genuine.

She tried to brush him off lightly: 'Nothing that bad. Just some hassle with Pat.'

'Pat?'

'The Housemother.'

He shot her a look which showed he wasn't altogether convinced, but didn't press the point and she was relieved. With his old easy grin he said: 'See you around then,' and drifted towards the crowd streaming out towards the drive, the gates, the buses. Home.

Gail stared out of the window for a long time without seeing uniformed kids, trees, birds or thunderpeaks gathering in purple-edged balloons over distant blocks of council flats.

'Thought you'd've gone by now.' Heather tapped Gail's shoulder. 'Glad you haven't though. We can catch the bus together. I suppose Milton's gone?' The last was put so casually that it was plain it meant a great deal. A spark of curiosity lit Gail's depressed mood.

'Yes. Why?'

'I wanted to ask him something, that's all. It'll keep.' Heather became very absorbed in the contents of her sprauncy bag, hair dropping like a blind across her face.

'Ask what?'

'Nothing...doesn't matter.'

'Sounds as though that's just what it does. You fancy him or something?' She let slip the dig out of pique and her own scratchy mood, not expecting the reaction she got.

'What if I do? What's wrong with that? What's it got to do with you or my parents or anybody else?' This so vehemently, Gail could only stare.

'No business of mine,' she agreed.

'Oh!' Heather's antagonism collapsed. She peered sheepishly through her veil of hair. 'That's all right then. Sorry. I thought...' but she didn't say what it was she thought, and slipping a confidential arm through Gail's as they left the House, added: 'There's something I've been meaning to ask you as a matter of fact. I'm having a bit of a do for my birthday and wondered if you'd like to come. Nothing high-flying. Just records and grub at my house. I wanted a proper disco but Mum and Dad were dead against it. Parents!' She hesitated. 'It's in a couple of weeks.'

So that was what she wanted Milton for – to ask him to her party! For herself, Gail didn't know whether to let her sneaking pleasure leak out, be upset, or give in completely and feel shattered. In all their years at school together, Heather had never once mentioned birthdays, let alone invited her to share. Which was okay. With their overtones of home and parents and being wanted, birthdays were happenings to be avoided if possible. When other kids gathered in knots to compare notes on parties, how much they drank, who puked, who'd had it away, she'd always taken care to be somewhere else, and Heather had tacitly seemed to understand. Now here she was, breaking the rules. Looking hopeful. *Wanting* her to come.

It was difficult saying: 'Thanks!' but Gail managed, thinking she'd had quite enough shocks to last her for several weeks.

But there were more to come.

At the gates, Heather gave her a nudge. 'Hey! Look.'

She looked and saw Brad and the ancient bike propped together on the grass verge at the roadside. Sunshine slipping through the leaves of the lime trees behind, dappled his blue shirt without softening a single inch of his craggy bulk. He was scowling at his feet. A ferocious, unapproachable, strangely imposing figure. Before she could cross the road and escape he looked up and saw her.

'Gail!'

She didn't want to go, but went – Heather in tow. The picture of Brad and old Penrose letting fly was crisply in her head and the nervousness that came surging up was a fine saw-toothed irritation.

What did he expect from her? There was nothing to talk about. She didn't care to think about gymnastics any more. Clamping her teeth together, she unconsciously imitated his scowl; bent on dowsing the little flame of hope which would keep burning. She was quite determined not to say a single word more than she could help.

He went straight to the point. 'About training. I've come to an arrangement with Mr Penrose. He refuses to let you back as an official club member till you've proved yourself. If you prove yourself, and only if, he'll reconsider. I've arranged with Mrs Price for you to use the school gym. She'll be there three nights a week. She's running a group for the Moderna stuff, so she'll keep an eye on you. The other two nights I'll manage. I've others to coach,' his glance included Heather, 'which means the timetabling'll be tight. Tonight is free for me, so I'd like you back here by five thirty sharp and we'll go over the programme I've worked out.' He stopped speaking as abruptly as he had begun. There was no hint he had even considered the possibility she might not want to fall in with these plans; no mention of the shouting match. Not a breath of any wish to hear her side of things.

As if he owns me, she thought, striving to sit on an immediate desire to tell him to get knotted. She belonged to herself and wasn't prepared to be owned by anyone. But he had succeeded in raising the old excitement. If she turned down the offer it would be for the sheer pleasure of a long distance slap at old Penrose and a kick at Brad's shins for his bossy manner – nothing else. Wordlessly she watched him wheel his bike into the road where he stopped, one foot on the pedal. A smile twitched his damaged cheek.

'Always supposing the arrangement suits,' he said, and waited.

She looked into the small hard grey eyes, refusing to be cowed this time. If he was granite she could be too. A smile she couldn't quite repress turned up the corners of her mouth.

'It suits.'

'I knew I'd not be wrong betting on you.' He pushed off, hooking his other leg over the saddle; free-wheeling away downhill before she had time to say anything more.

Heather burst out laughing. 'You should just see your face! If looks could kill he'd be a stiff by now.'

'Crap,' Gail said absently.

'It's true. You and old Penrose – champion eye-slaughterers! On second thoughts I'd back him to win. I tell you, you were well out of it last night. After you'd bolted they made us *work*. No more shouting or anything, just this freezing politeness routine. Nobody dared put a toe wrong. Holy mackerel, it was enough to give you the galloping squits!'

They had been walking through the first rumbles of thunder, and now rain began to spit. Heather turned up her collar. 'Penrose is a mean old fart not letting you come back,' she concluded as they reached the bus stop. 'But he'll have to in the end. You'll see. It isn't the same without you there.'

Gail, who had been mildly amused by Heather's description of Penrose, was astonished, never having thought her presence in the gym had affected anyone, least of all Heather. She felt confused.

A spear of lightning split the sky, now the colour of lead. The rain changing from fine needles to a pelting downpour, splashed up like small fountains as the bus glided towards the kerb.

'In the nick of time too,' Heather said.

Still juggling with her astonishment, Gail followed her on to the bus.

6

The school gym was almost empty as Gail went in to a burst of syncopated music. A couple of girls were pulling ropes from their training bags. A third was practising with a red plastic ball – throwing, catching, throwing again high as she twisted, knelt and tried to be in time to catch again. And failed. Brad, lounging in one of the tubular steel and blue canvas chairs, watched with critical frowning concentration.

The music switched off abruptly. With the recorder before her on a table, Mrs Price changed cassettes. Tried the new one briefly, switched off, ran the tape fast, then tried it again. She nodded to Gail walking across the gym.

Brad looked up without moving. 'Ah! So you've come.'

Gail's spine went ramrod straight. 'Did you think I wouldn't?'

'Couldn't be sure, could I? Don't know you that well... yet!' His glance was diamond hard and sharp enough to cut. 'It'll be different before we've finished I daresay.' Without further explanation he got off the chair, asking her if she'd had anything to eat and what it was.

'Beans on toast, flapjacks, a mug of tea.' A sketchy meal, consumed in a hurry.

'How much sugar?'

'Two spoons.' She understood very well why he was asking and expected a telling off. She was fat as a boiled dumpling.

The good eyebrow went up. He stuffed his hands into the double pocket on the front of his track top. 'If I was to ask you what gymnastic aims you have, what would you say?'

That you're potty if you expect me to do a big scene opening up my heart and all that crap, Gail thought, and was silent.

'I don't care how much of a pipe dream it is. Spit it out. Just so long as it's the truth.'

Granite, she reminded herself, and met the scouring eyes with a shrug.

His acute observation of her didn't waver an inch. 'There's no sense in resisting. Let's get one thing straight from the word go. If you want help then you've got to give some. You ought to know that. You've done enough. It's a two-way business and anyone who puts on blinkers is a fool. And don't think I'm asking out of idle curiosity. As your coach I need to know. There's got to be complete honesty between us. That's the foundation. Make it of sand and we're sunk.'

There was an intensity in the way he spoke, as if driven by an inner heat, which stirred her. Some of the hard resistance crumbled, but not all. She saw Natasha Malinova thin and defiant on the Olympic rostrum, bending her head as the wide ribbon of an Olympic Gold was slipped over her dark hair. Standing straight when the Russian Anthem blared and died into a thunder of applause. Only it wasn't Malinova, it was herself. She *couldn't* blab all that, it was far too corny! What did he take her for? The very thought made her guts ravel and knot like old parcel string.

'And the higher your aims the better. Doesn't matter a rap whether or not you think you have a gnat in hell's chance of achieving them. If they are there and you feel committed right down inside the very heart of you, then we've a point to work from. And if you *do*,' he added, 'then that's a bonus. The icing on the celebration cake. And by heck we'll make it a celebration you'll never forget!' He chuckled suddenly; surprisingly. A disarming sound which got under her guard. Against her will she felt drawn to him, liking his bluntness, his disregard for polite chat and the building of walls to hide behind like most people did. He was different from anyone she had ever met. But she was worried, having sworn not to get involved with people on a deep level again. Now he was saying that if she was to be a gymnast proper, she had to go back on all that.

But some small inner spring seemed to have been released. She wanted to confide. Almost had the nerve. Not quite.

When she didn't speak, he said more gently: 'There's no shame in having high aims. It's to your credit.'

Hesitation. Then: 'A FIG pin,' she said in a rush, glance flickering away, but going back directly.

One side of his mouth twitched up in a smile. He held out his hand. Slowly she put hers into it and felt the dry iron grasp. 'It's a high flier who comes home from an International match with one of those,' he said. 'But I was asking for all the truth, not half.'

She could escape neither from his iron grip nor his watching waiting penetrating eyes. It was terrible. She was being relentlessly turned inside out. The demand was too much. She wouldn't... couldn't put up her innermost self to be mocked at.

'Come on then!'

No escape.

'A Gold medal.'

He waited, still holding.

'An Olympic Gold medal.' It was out. She felt limp as a squeezed flannel.

Brad said softly: 'Aye lass, I suspected you'd aim for the top!' He let go her hand, keeping any personal reactions to himself.

But he hasn't scoffed, she thought with colossal relief. No polite hints either about wild daydreaming or being out of my class. She almost laughed. Brad would never be polite! He'd said – No blinkers; complete honesty. So perhaps that meant...

She stamped on the train of thought. It wasn't new, but for the first time was lit with magic possibility, which she daren't examine. She didn't want this tiny hope snuffed out so soon. It would be snuffed out. Deep down she knew it. Things always were. But not yet.

Brad took her by the shoulders, pinning her with his frowning gaze. 'You know what it means, don't you? *Nothing is more important than training!*' He emphasized each word. 'So no nights off with your boyfriend to go to discos or the pictures. *Training comes first,*' again leaning on each word.

'I haven't got a boyfriend,' thinking of Steve.

'Just as well with the programme I've mapped out for you.' He fished a notebook from his pocket. 'Reckon they need their eyes testing.'

She didn't take in his meaning until he was well launched into the schedule for improving her fitness. Then a blush worked up her neck, roasting her cheeks. She was relieved he was busy jotting down a list of food to avoid, exercises to follow – which began as before with six laps of the gym as a warm-up.

'Not risking injuries, especially right at the beginning of the season. I want you fighting fit for the Women's Individual Apparatus Championships.'

Her mouth sagged. He'd not been kidding when he'd spoken of complete honesty. Only he should have said – complete honesty and *craziness*! If he thought she could be ready to try so soon for this top women's championship he was as much of a nutter as she was.

'How soon is it?'

'Mid December.'

She felt breathless; scatty; her mind doing kangaroo jumps from one mad thought to another, but over all a lightheartedness she couldn't put down.

47

'You've quite enough competition experience under your belt to make this a perfectly reasonable scheme. So don't look at me as if I'm sending you direct to the Olympics!' He twisted her round and slapped her between the shoulder blades. 'Get going.'

She went – gasping! But as her body fell into a rhythm, so did her bounding thoughts. A few facts emerged.

She was back.

One major dream was in the open.

Brad hadn't given himself a hernia laughing. She was to aim for the Individuals... It was enough to be going on with.

She finished the sixth lap and began the long process of suppling rusty shoulder muscles by drawing large circles in the air with her arms.

7

'And when I tried talking to her about going on this diet, you wouldn't believe the fuss she made – that's when I finally managed to get her to stand still for a couple of seconds.'

'Why's that?'

'I dunno. Thinks I'm heading for a bout of anorexia whatsit or something.' With a dramatic gesture, Gail flung an arm across her forehead. 'She'll be a walking skeleton. She'll catch everything going. She'll die poor little mite!'

Heather giggled. Gail pulled a face of resigned despair and dabbing a finger on an escaped bun crumb, rolled it into a pellet and flicked hard. It landed centrally in Heather's plastic beaker of coffee, sinking without trace.

'Oh thank *you*!'

'Anytime.'

'What else did she say then?'

'It's too *crumby* to tell!' Gail joined in Heather's mock groan, laughed with her, then relapsed back into gloom, eyes fixed on the entwined initials RW and FC inside a heart which had been scratched into the wooden table top.

'She means well of course. In fact she's quite nice really. But what else is there left to do except starve? And then she starts making these little backhanded snipes about wasting food. Housemothers!'

'She can't make you eat.' Heather nibbled the edge of an unbuttered Ryvita biscuit. 'Perhaps she hasn't cottoned on to you having a real purpose. She probably thinks it's just a fad. Maybe you didn't explain properly.'

'Yes I have. I told you! But it's like talking to that wall

over there.' Gail waved an impatient hand indicating the orange emulsion edged with purple – a recent decorative flight of fancy done by a few fifth-form enthusiasts to improve their personal common-room. 'I tell you she never *listens*. She's always doing about fifty different things all at the same time. You can just see there's a sort of glazed look in her eyes. "Yes dear . . . no dear . . . three bags full dear . . ." *And* she paints her toenails. I hate people who paint their toenails!' She finished fiercely, as if it was the ultimate horror.

Heather, whose toenails were at that moment Stardust Pearl, was temporarily silenced. She took a gulp of coffee, then set the beaker carefully back into its wet ring on the table, privately convinced that Gail was making too much of it all.

'No breakfast today,' Gail went on. 'Porridge and toast . . . I ask you!'

Heather held out a Ryvita biscuit which was accepted. 'What about that Mrs Thingummy – you know, the woman you see every now and again at the office?'

'Mrs Bridgeman – the social worker you mean?'

'That's her. Can't you ask her to put in a good word?'

Through a muffle of half-chewed biscuit, Gail said: 'You have to be joking! Know what she's like? A haggis tarted up in a potato sack with string round the middle. And she booms. The most intimate details about your knickers not being tidied away and why you go on being so bloody unco-operative, get blasted all over the building. No ta! I see her when I have to. That's me lot!'

It was said jokingly, but Heather felt a pang of sympathy. Although the last weeks had drawn them much closer together, she knew it was more than her life was worth to show anything that smacked of pity. She offered the only acceptable morsel of comfort she could dig up.

'If you think you're overweight, take a look at me. Ten ton Tessie!'

'We're different types. I'm Ectomorph. You are En-domorph,' Gail said, as if this absolved Heather from her extra pounds.

'Good grief! What's that?'

'Skinny and...'

'Fat,' Heather filled in mournfully as Gail hesitated. 'Which is my point. So what are you griping about? Have another Ryvita and shut up.'

'It's your last.'

'Just as well. Look!' She grabbed a handful of her well-covered waist and squeezed. With her back to the door she hadn't seen Milton come in.

He said: 'Hi!' leaning over her shoulder to get a better view of what she was doing, his hair brushing her cheek.

Heather's hands shot from her waist as if it was red hot. She went scarlet, seized her beaker gulping the remains of coffee so fast that she choked.

Milton thumped her unhelpfully on the back.

In the flurry of coughing, Gail got up. Milton must be blind if he can't see how she feels about him, she thought. The way she looks whenever he appears. Why can't she have more pride? She can't know she's doing it. Gail felt a pang of pity. Perhaps she should give him a hint? She gave up the idea as soon as it was born, knowing that Heather would spit blood if she did. Even the pity had to be buried.

Milton, having made the situation worse by changing his hefty thumps to gentler more sympathetic pats, sat down in a chair next to Heather, saying to Gail:

'Aren't going are you? I've some news for you.'

Gail asked: 'What?' still standing.

'I've been doing a bit of detective work.' His voice was cheerful and extra loud to combat the cacophony of voices and radio pop. 'It's that old bird,' he went on. 'You know – her that was a nurse like me Mum. Mrs Box? Remember all those relations I was telling you about?

51

Well the girl who married her brother, her maiden name was Knight!'

It took Gail a moment to follow what he was on about. She got there then sat down abruptly because her knees gave and because it was important he didn't go on talking so loud. She tried to be casual.

'So what. There's hundreds of Knights. Look in the phone book.'

'Daresay there are. But that's not the point.'

She knew he was only being friendly, but she was furious with him for blundering in all cheerful and well-meaning. 'Why don't you mind your own business,' she snapped, before she could catch the words and stuff them back.

A small hollow of silence formed inside the noise. Heather filled it.

'D'you mind telling me what all this is about?'

'It was about nothing at all. Milton was sticking his nose in where it isn't wanted,' Gail said and dumped her training bag down on the long form next to Mrs Capucelli's table. She had managed to avoid answering at school, but had been nabbed as soon as she stuck her head round the door of the gym at the Sports Centre.

'Oh come on! Anyone with half an eye can see you're fretting. And its bad for you,' Heather insisted.

'Bad for you y'mean!' Gail unzipped her bag, took out a pair of worn gymnastic slippers and rezipped it with unnecessary force. 'You're as nosy as him. You make a good pair.'

Heather muttered: 'Wish we did,' turning away.

Gail sighed. Heather's sensitivity where Milton was concerned was becoming a drag. She wondered if it was a drag to Milton, and felt a flicker of sympathy. He wasn't thick. He must know. And if he knew and wasn't going to ask her to go out with him, that meant only one thing.

Poor Heather! It was altogether too difficult seeing both sides. She sighed again. 'I didn't mean...' She decided to speak out in the hopes of getting Heather to shut up and let her give her mind to the training session to come. 'If you remember, the sister-in-law was black. That's what he was on about. Now d'you see?'

'She might be family you mean?' Heather looked up from tying her laces, beaming. 'How exciting. Long lost family.'

Gail groaned. The thing had backfired. 'No it's not.'

'Why?' Heather was genuinely surprised.

'If *you* didn't have family and someone came up with a stray white Stafford, how would you react?'

Heather thought about this. 'To make it right I'd have to be an orphan living in Africa. Then I'd take an interest in your stray white Stafford. Cor! It'd be thrilling. Fancy, no family, then a whole lot landing in your lap. People you'd never known, who'd been around all the time.'

This was more than Gail could take. 'Oh for crying out loud, what romantic crap! Anyroad, you heard what he said before. She's dead. They're all dead.' She felt disturbed, uneasy. Mind shifting away from what she was here to do. She frowned; tried to change the subject. 'I didn't know that Milton's mum was a nurse.'

'Oh I knew,' Heather said. 'And his dad's a bus driver.'

Gail's frown deepened. She'd missed out again. Just as she'd missed out about Milton's reggae band and that he played guitar. Did she go round with her eyes shut and her ears buttoned like Milton said? She had never thought of herself like that. What had she thought? What did she want? The answer wasn't so immediate as before. Then it had been clear-cut – Olympic Gold and Parents. Now? The Olympic Gold was still there, a fantastic towering dream, but the obstacles between were legion. Insurmountable. And Parents?

But she couldn't do with that hassle now. There were

other more pressing things. Tonight was supremely important. Her first attack on the apparatus since Brad had
dreamed up the gruelling three-week refitness programme.
She owed it to him to do well. He had got her back into
favour with Penrose, which only mattered because it gave
her the chance to work with proper apparatus. And it
wasn't exactly favour. More a grudging armed truce, but
enough to be going on with.

If I step out of line though, she thought, I'll be booted
from here to next week, never to return. Well, he won't
have the pleasure. Any minute now, she realized, spotting
Bob Penrose talking to Cathy by the asymmetrics. She
looked round. Denise was here too. And Mrs Capucelli,
talking to a small girl, as she searched through the pile of
leotards. The girl had a pigtail pinned straight up the
back of her head like a Red Indian feather. She stood
there, small and shut-in, waiting. A very new training bag
was clutched in both hands. Gail had a vivid memory of
herself, small and shut-in, waiting. It seemed like a
hundred years since that first day in the after-school gym
club held in her junior school. Excitement began now as
then in the region of her stomach, shooting out along veins
and nerves until it hit her skin. A jittery electric-shock feeling, which lasted through the warm-up and into the
apparatus work.

They had divided into groups, Cathy, Heather and herself, a separate advanced trio on the asymmetric bars.
Limbering her spine, Gail watched Brad coaching Cathy.
A scowl of concentration made his expression distant and
ruthless. A total contrast to Jackie Wells who had been
rarely severe and rather giggly. Gail felt apprehensive;
keyed up almost to competition pitch. Yearning to do well,
but afraid of failure. Penrose had disappeared. Bet he'll
turn up again just as soon as I get started, she thought,
looking back at Brad who was still scowling. Not a trace of
the humour that would sometimes break into the worst

54

moments of the relentless training pressure and save her from hating him. He was like two people. Fierce one moment, joking the next. Even his face had two distinct sides. And behind both was this driving force that never let up. She could feel it now, an almost physical power, zooming across the few yards of matting which separated them.

She touched her toes; straightened up, fidgeting with the foam padding under her leotard, then put hands on hips, circling from the waist up. Her hands felt soft — tender where the newly healed blister was on the pad below her little finger. The hard skin was a thing of the past. But she only had to be patient and it would soon be as grainy as the soles of her feet. Everything would come back. It must... all of it! She slipped on her handguards.

'Who is that over there with old Penrose?' Heather whispered in her ear.

Gail looked across the gym to the door and saw a small poker-backed woman with fair hair stylishly cropped to reveal a well-shaped head. She was draped becomingly in plain cream jersey which flowed round her stocky body: the plainness touched off by a knotted waist-length scarf of brown silk.

'Haven't a clue.'

There was no time to speculate as Cathy was already swinging down from the upper bar. Her nutcracker dismount lost its flow and was marred as she snagged a toe on the mat, pitching on to her knees. Brad's frown deepened. A flush stained her round cheeks and Gail knew exactly how she felt. Her own face burned as she pushed the Reuther board into place, then went to the magnesium bowl to dust her hands and handguards.

A long run-up, a thump down on the board and she shot to the upper bar, pulling up, resting across at an angle. Even with the foam padding the hard wood bruised her pelvic bone. She was as soft as a teddy bear! Curling up she circled the bar in a ball. A swing back and up. Switching to a straddle support with the strain of it making her arms quiver. But she wasn't going to give in! Rolling over; suspended in a long hang below the bar, arms crying out again ... and again with the upstart. She'd do it or die! Swing; release; catch; piked handstand; tuck ...

What should have been fluid continuous movement was the rust bound jerking of a clockwork toy left out too long in the rain. Terrible! But she didn't stop. Or fall off. Or snag a toe. The landing too, came with a solid comforting unbudging smack.

Three pairs of cool assessing eyes confronted her. The faces of Penrose and the cream jersey woman relaxed almost to the point of a smile, but not quite.

Brad said: 'Could've been worse, considering.'

Thanks very much you grudging old sod, Gail thought, breathless and limp but underneath aware of a sneaking pleasure. He wasn't famous for ladling out the compliments and she was content not to have been panned, knowing she'd not once lost her body awareness in relation to the bars, or felt hesitation. She had worked with every ounce of herself. No fear.

'You need to position yourself better on the upper bar when you first pull up.' Brad angled a beefy forearm. 'You're making a bad leg shape – bending your knees ... see?'

'Yes.' Satisfaction slipped. It had been a creaky unrehearsed routine. A flop. The long lay-off was no excuse.

'Let's be having you back again. Don't bother with the run-up.' He lifted her by the hips, hooking her on to the upper bar like a monkey, calling out: 'Better ... better ... NO!' as she bungled a hand catch and had to scrabble to save herself from falling. 'Try again.' He re-hung her. She pulled up again with screaming arms.

'No!' Again he stopped her. 'You aren't thinking of every inch. See yourself, lass. See it there,' he laid a finger between her eyebrows. 'And again ... that's *it*!' as she pulled and swung and panted, striving to make the rusty muscles obey, then missing the final catch as she moved between bars, because sweat had defeated the magnesium dust and her hands were sore and slippery. She collapsed in a heap, banging her hip and awkwardly twisting an ankle.

'Are you okay?' He was squatting beside her, grasping the leg and manipulating the ankle with expert fingers almost before she had time to draw breath.

She screwed up her face. 'Ow!'

But he only grinned. 'Try standing.'

She did, hating him briefly. The ankle felt bruised; nothing more.

'Reckon you'll live till next time, lass. Only watch that grasp. Shoulder width and no wider. Understand?'

She nodded once.

'Right. Now we'll see if you can't do as well with your Floor exercise.'

'And *that* compliment,' Heather said when the session was over and they were walking across the bridge into the snack bar, "should keep you going for the next six weeks. Fancy a bag of crisps?'

'At half a stone overweight? You're joking! I've got to face sarnies tomorrow on that Bristol trip.' Gail was talking about food, but her mind was labouring over the Floor exercise which Jackie had helped her devise and which had suddenly seemed badly put together. Dull. One quick flip round the mat had proved it. She hadn't needed anyone to tell her, though it had been written all over their faces. And the opinion of the cream jersey woman had turned out to be even more important than old Penrose's. She was Mrs Frost, organizer of the Zone squad – only one notch down from the National squad, those archangels who represented Britain in all the big International matches. Mrs Frost was on the lookout for new talent. Gail's mind was still reeling. She felt overawed; full of longing and desperate despair. If only she hadn't wasted those precious summer weeks mooning over the loss of Steve and Jackie! What did they matter? What did anything matter compared with her ambition to be the very best.

'I'll bring Ryvita for two tomorrow,' Heather said.

'Ryvita?' Her head was dizzy with so many ballooning hopes. Knowing they had no more substance than dreams didn't make any difference. She couldn't hold them down. *'Ryvita?'*

'Yes, Ryvita. You know, that brown biscuity stuff that looks like cardboard. Where were you? Marching down the arena at Crystal Palace, heading the National squad?'

The joke fell too near home. 'Okay, bring two and I'll eat yours as well.'

'You can abandon your calory counts on my birthday, not before. Which reminds me... I've got to postpone the orgy. Gran's been ill and she's convalescing at our house. We have to be quiet!' She pulled a long face. 'So the party'll be when she's gone. I'll let you know the new date as soon as it's decided.'

In the foyer Gail pushed open the glass door, letting Heather out and the dusky breeze in, her mind almost entirely occupied with trying to beat the problem of the Floor exercise.

8

The first thing that met Gail's eyes as they went up the steps and in through the swing doors was a large 'Boxkite' aeroplane suspended from the high ceiling. A frail delicate contraption that looked as if one gust of wind would smash it to pieces. It was the original of a model Steve Miller had made, and the sight of it was so unexpected she could only stand and gape. She realized with a jolt, that she hadn't given him more than a passing thought for ages. He'd had several weeks of Borstal now. Shut in. She shivered.

'Don't tell me they used things like that for carting slaves!' Heather said.

'Two at a time? They'd've needed a whole fleet.' Gail copied her flippancy, trying to throw off the haunting thoughts of Steve.

They were in the entrance hall of Bristol Museum. A party of twenty-five, brought by coach on a drizzly morning by Jimmy Lomas and another history teacher, Mrs Gregory, whom Gail till then had only known by sight. The museum was large, light and handsomely marbled, the hall having an inquiry kiosk by one door and a counter for books, postcards and gifts opposite. In the centre was the exhibition featuring the slave trade. A collection of display boards and glass cases set against a huge aerial diagram of a slaving ship sliced through, revealing row upon row of slaves packed like canned fish.

'Two hundred and ninety-two.' Milton turned from counting to look at the 'Boxkite'. Give me air travel any day. Fancy a flip in that?'

Gail tried to imagine herself in the fragile structure, flying through whistling wind. 'Reckon so,' she said doubtfully. The idea of canvas and wire and not much else between her and the ground was alarming, but not as unpleasant as being wedged shoulder to shoulder like the slaves in the ship. She thought of them chained down, being tossed around in a storm and wondered what they had done if they were seasick or wanted to pee.

Milton was still gazing at the 'Boxkite' apparently untroubled by such ideas.

'You must be round the twist if you'd trust yourself to a glorified matchbox like that!' Heather said.

'Well if some people hadn't, none of us would be jetting to Spain or Teneriffe for holidays,' Milton pointed out.

'Oh yeah and which of us does that then? Skeggy is as far as we ever get.' Heather's voice was mocking, but her eyes betrayed her.

She's dotty about him, Gail thought. Dewy-eyed; adoring – can't he see?

Milton blew on his fingernails and rubbed them on his denim shirt, apparently oblivious of the effect he was having. 'Went to visit me auntie in Kingston last Easter.'

Gail was impressed. She had never been outside England in the whole of her life. The thought was suddenly confining and she was filled with a longing to travel. Gymnastic teams travelled. If she could do well...be picked...

She thrust away the daydreams and walked to one of the display boards staring intently. There was a series of photoprints of etchings, quaintly old-fashioned, which disguised the reality of corpses dangling from trees, huddles of half-clothed people, branding scenes. In a glass-topped case a few roughly forged tools for shackling and branding were laid side by side with an assortment of other devices for torture.

They look *used*, she thought, disturbed – wondering if

the Great-Great Milton had mentioned had been branded or had some other terrible thing done to him? Perhaps one of these very bits of old iron had burned into his flesh or forced open his mouth. She shivered again.

'Lovely ideas them fellers had.' Milton looked over her shoulder.

'Makes me want to spew.'

'Imagine that thing in your own gob!' He sounded almost jaunty as he pointed to the mouth clamp.

She saw with a small shock that he was grinning. 'Don't it get at your guts?' she asked.

'Nope.'

It wasn't the reaction she had expected. 'But they used them things on real people. People like that Great-Great you were talking about. Don't that make it seem real to you? Can't you imagine it happening?'

'Course I can. That's not the point. The Great-Great is dead. Can't feel nothing now.'

'That's a bit callous.'

Milton shrugged. 'It's living flesh and blood I cares about.'

'What d'you mean?'

He stared as if she puzzled him. 'The now. People – now. World's full of 'em. Brothers, grandads, aunties ... you name 'em. Enough to fret over without having to cry for dead folk.'

She said tersely: 'I wouldn't know would I?'

'I don't mean just blood relatives,' he said quickly.

She was unreasonably irritated. 'Who else cares?'

He laughed. 'Come off it! You don't have to be *related* to care.'

'That's nothing but words. You can say anything with words. It don't make it real.' Was he trying it on? A crappy joke? Or was he sincere? 'Look out for yourself. No one else will,' she finished.

'Then what?' He suddenly lost his easy going manner

and frowned at her. 'Be shoved around from here to break-fast time? Don't give me that! Stick together ... care ... or we're sunk. Life's too short anyroad.'

At a loss, she gave the first answer that came into her head: 'You may be. Not me!'

Milton dug his hands into the pockets of his jeans. 'Jesus! Stuff your head into the sand ...'

She bristled. 'And what's that supposed to mean?'

He gave her a long hard unrelenting look. 'If you must know I'm talking about honkies beating us up. Telling us to go back where we came from and worse. Surely you've had some?'

Us, Gail thought. Us! Us! Us! She was dumbfounded, yet knew she ought not to be. There was nothing strange in Milton assuming she had experienced things like this. Being called Cadbury for instance. It seemed a paltry example. But there must have been other things, other times? Was it possible not to notice? All her life she'd been obsessed about who her parents were, mother especially; who she was. Never a thought for *what*! She must be thick as a plank not to have bothered with the *what* side of things before. He could be right saying she spent her time running from things unpleasant. A glance showed her that he was still studying her intently. She shrivelled inside, wanted to run, wanted then to laugh at herself for doing the very thing he mocked. Honkies! A term of contempt. She looked down at the back of her hands, slowly turning them over. Brown and pink with fine lines joining the two colours. So – she was part honky part black. Did that make her an outcast from both sides? And why did there have to be sides?

'Well haven't you?' he insisted.

She didn't know what to say. They were standing close, but not touching. Now, someone squeezing in for a better look at the display case behind shoved them together, saving her from having to answer. Her nose brushed his denim shirt. She felt the rise and fall of his diaphragm. The smell of clean ironed cotton, fresh sweat, warm skin, met her like a physical assault which took her breath and her anger. When she could, she backed away, chattering to cover her embarrassment.

'Talk about the London rush hour! Just like when Heather and me got took to Earl's Court once for a gymnastic meeting. Hanging on them straps in the tube train was as good as playing at ham sarnies...the *crush*!' She remembered that someone had pinched her bum...

Like now!

She dug back with her elbow, twisting round. Gray was leering at her, the great moon of Craig's face resting on his shoulder.

'Seen your namesake, Cadbury?' Craig asked.

She gave them an icicle stare.

'No kidding!' He raised his fists high enough for her to see, jigging up and down on rhinoceros toes. 'Seconds out!'

'Oh drop dead!' They were a pain in the backside with their everlasting corny remarks. She moved to escape, but Craig stopped her.

'I'm not joking. Go and see for yourself.'

'I can't can I, with you in the way.'

'Leave off, Fatso. Come this way, Gail.' Milton stepped back from the display case to let her pass, but Craig, scowling, closed in. There was some shoulder shoving and muttered curses. Gail, trapped between, took a hasty step back for balance and came up against one of the display boards making it judder and shift. As luck would have it, Jimmy Lomas was on the other side. He appeared like a bristling hedgehog, cindery voice demanding to know what they thought they were playing at?

Craig, Gray, Milton, Heather, a couple of onlookers, all started explaining at once:

'It was him sir...*he* pushed *me*...other way round

63

y'mean...you started it...I never...yes he did I saw...
liar, nothing to see... was... wasn't...'

'Would you kindly SHUT UP!' Jimmy barked, and the
half-spoken sentences froze in the air. He glared at them
in turn, gaze resting longer on Gail than the rest. 'I spend
my time and energies organizing a trip to help you with
your studies and what do you do? Behave like infants in
nappies instead of supposedly responsible fifth-formers.
Exams are looming. We haven't come here for a gay
time...'

A snigger of laughter brought him up short. Blood
rushed along the cords of his neck and his gooseberry eyes
bulged slightly. He gathered himself with obvious effort.
'I'm glad you can find something to laugh at. To help
your levity you can be outside the staff room tomorrow at
four sharp and I'll explain fully. Now get back and see if
you can put your minds to learning. L.E.A.R.N.I.N.G.
We aren't here for a rest-cure. Move!'

Not quite out of earshot, Heather snorted. 'Load of fuss
over nothing! Anybody 'ud think you knocked the damn
thing for six.' She glowered at the last and nearest display
board on which hung a poster glassed and framed in gilt.
'Did you see the look he gave you... as if it was all your
fault?'

Gail had but didn't want to chew the cud. She felt
muddled and uneasy. As if someone had taken her mind
to pieces and thrown the bits in a heap. Not because of
Jimmy's outburst – if no one had laughed he would have
growled and left it at that – it stemmed from the conversation with Milton. 'Lomas isn't worth getting in a muck
sweat about,' she said, looking at the crude drawings of
two bare knuckle-fighters, one black, one white. The old
block type was very worn and not easy to read.

'But it's so unfair. He's got his knife into you.'

'That one looks like Milton.' Gail deliberately turned
the conversation, leaning forward and reading out:

'BUTCHER splodge WILL THIS splodge FIGHT IN splodge
ROUNDS, MIDNIGHT THE splodge BLACK FROM THE GUINEA
splodge.'

Heather was pink and giggling. Whether from the mention of Milton or her reading, Gail didn't know or care.
She had succeeded in getting off the subject of Lomas,
school and everything to do with both. At that moment
she felt she would have given anything to get in the old
'Boxkite' and fly away.

It was not until they had toured the rest of the museum
and were about to leave for the coach and Clifton Downs,
that Gail realized what Craig had been talking about.

Stapled to the bottom of the display board underneath
the poster was an oblong of white card. Typed on it:

LATE EIGHTEENTH CENTURY – loaned by Mrs Jarman
Knight.

She read on:

Jem Tudge, a miner from the Kingswood district, well known in
his day as a fighter of merit, was defeated at the above contest
by the ex-slave Midnight (African name – Olaudah), a distant
relative of the late Mr Jarman Knight. Midnight came to England as a personal servant to the captain of a slaving ship. Like
other slaves arriving in England after 1773, he was automati-
cally freed and subsequently went on to a highly successful but
brief career as a bare-knuckle fighter before disappearing.
Nothing is known of his later life.

She read it twice.

The rest of the school party bought postcards and were
gathering to leave.

She read it a third time. Looked up. Saw the group.
Hurried to the counter where she chose a birthday card
for Heather. Hesitated. Chose another to give to herself,
and bought both. Looked for Heather, but seeing her next
to Milton, went out of the museum alone.

9

They came away from the staff room late, plodding down the stairs. Nobody spoke till they were outside. Then Craig turned on Milton.

'You wait, Pepper. I'll flatten you y'lanky git!'

Milton was unperturbed. 'What are you so uptight about? It's only an hour's extra homework.'

'An hour I haven't got. There's all the other stuff ...remember?'

'So?'

'So I've got other things to do.'

'He's right. Me an' all,' Gray said.

'It's only an hour,' Milton repeated mildly.

'If you say that again I'll shut your gob for you permanent!' Craig showed him a fist.

Gail said sharply: 'Oh belt up! If anyone's short of time it's Heather and me.' A pile of worries nagged at her – the Floor exercise, the Apparatus Championships, a backlog of other homework, the threeway problem of Milton, Heather and herself. Life was becoming impossible.

Gray looked sour. 'What makes you and her so special, Cadbury?'

Milton slipped her a quick smile. She was instantly pleased. Instantly wished she didn't care. She said: 'Not special – busy. We've both got to train.'

'Think you're the only ones?'

She was surprised. 'What d'you train for then ... soccer?'

'Karate.' Gray jerked his thumb at Craig. 'He's going for his blue belt next week,' and turning back to Milton, 'so you'd better look out, Pepper. He weren't kidding.'

'Why don't you shut your mouth,' Gail snapped. 'You don't do nothing but talk.'

'And why don't you go back where you came from...him too! You don't belong here.' Gray was suddenly furious.

Gail couldn't speak. It was unfair. Cruel! A stab in the gut. She heard Heather saying loudly:

'What a load of old rubbish! Where should she go? She's English as you Gray Wilkins. And why shouldn't Milton live here? He's got as much right as anybody. You're a stupid prat!' She tucked her arm into Gail's.

Weakened even more by this unexpected support, Gail allowed herself to be pulled away. By the time they reached Arden House she had recovered, but while collecting her books the other worries returned. The homework load was already unmanageable. Now this extra from Lomas. How could she get everything done without being late for training? Being prompt, like giving all of yourself to every movement, was an essential part of gymnastics. She couldn't fail so soon after the painful trek back. Wouldn't give Brad the slenderest chance to snarl and say she was slacking.

There seemed only one way.

'I shan't do it,' she told Heather.

'He'll go bananas!'

'Better him than me.' She heaved her bag off the floor, pretending to an indifference and nerve she didn't feel. 'If he says anything I shall tell him what he can do!'

On one knee, hands outstretched behind in what should have been an elegant balletic shape suggesting a swan, Gail finished the Floor exercise.

It was a disaster. More like an imitation of Donald Duck. And hunger didn't help. Missing tea in order to get to the club on time was all very well, but there hadn't been a moment's chance to phone Pat and explain that she'd stayed on at school to do the extra homework. Which meant she would be in the cactus when she got back. And all because she was chicken! She should have told Jimmy what he could do like she'd said.

Miserable and dissatisfied, she stood up. The tumbling had been awful. Creaky cartwheels. Heavy pirouettes. Leaps pathetic. Even the dance steps and rhythm, usually a strong point, had fallen apart.

'Again,' Brad called. 'Cut the first open stream of tumbling. Take it from here.' He wound back the tape and reset it at a slower passage where the piano vamped through several sentimental bars, motioning to Gail to position herself.

Mutinously she stuck out her right foot, pointing the toes, arms behind, hands half curled. A new style Donald Duck. If she could squawk as well it would be more in character. Liven things up a bit. Couldn't he see it was hopeless?

The rerun was no better. She would have felt sourly triumphant if she hadn't been so depressed and anxious.

Brad clicked off the recorder. Said: 'Mmm!' and frowned.

She understood his reaction precisely. A small burst of told-you-so feeling was quickly replaced by a brick-heavy sensation settling on her empty stomach. 'Was it that lousy?'

'Yes.'

At least he never hedged. The scene was grim with the Apparatus Championship only seven weeks off. She said: 'It's the music. I don't feel it.'

'I thought you chose it?'

'No.'

'Who then?'

'Miss ... *Mrs* Kerr.'

'Why the hell didn't you say you weren't happy with her choice before putting in all that work?'

68

Why indeed, Gail wondered! Now it seemed crackers not to have done so, but at the time things had somehow been different. Jackie had a way of coaxing people round to her own views without them knowing. To say now that she had always thought the music sounded out of date would be wet. More wet still to admit she'd put off thinking about it. Not knowing what to say, she shrugged.

Brad gave her one of his piercing sceptical looks, took in a deep breath, then let out the air through his flattened boxer's nose an inch at a time. 'I see!'

She was afraid he did. Too much.

'Well there's no point in flogging a dead horse. Better to start again from scratch.' He glanced at his watch, the class, back at Gail, as if aware of time slipping away. 'Seven weeks to the Individuals.'

'I know.'

'And what's your choice?'

'Reggae?' She was startled into misunderstanding.

'I wasn't asking about music, but you've answered me. I won't say Reggae's no good, but I don't know that there's enough variety of rhythm for what you need.'

She was nettled. 'It's the rhythm I like.'

'Good rhythm in a lot of stuff. How about jazz?'

'Don't like it much,' she said stubbornly.

'Know any?' he asked, equally stubborn.

'Not much.' The Reggae beat was in her head. In her bones. It felt right. She thought of Milton – and his group. Perhaps he could suggest some way of getting round the rhythm problem. Maybe make a tape? She could drop round at his band practice after the club. Only it wasn't that easy, she realized. There were other considerations. Milton might get the wrong idea.

She looked at Heather on the edge of the floor-matting, practising a back flip. Doing it with grace. Heather had improved remarkably, she saw with sudden surprise. But then Heather was still part of the Elite group that had extra coaching up at the College gym on Saturdays. How long before old Penrose would give in and let *her* go back to the Elite group, she wondered with a stab of envy. Next thing she'd hear was that Heather had been selected for the Zone squad. She swam up from these thoughts and did some ear unbuttoning, noticing that Brad was looking at her as if expecting an answer to some question.

'Sorry?'

'I said – do you belong to the record library?'

'Yes ... no. Mrs Kerr did.'

'You've got to do a lot of listening. Discover what you like; what moves you physically.' He glanced at Heather waiting now to begin her Floor routine. 'Tell you what – I've a fair selection of records. If you can get to my flat straight after school tomorrow there should be time to try a few. Flaxhill Road. Know it?'

'Yes.' She was intrigued by the idea of nosing out his home life, but resistant to having him stand over her while she tried to pick out suitable pieces of music. She'd agree to anything, just to get away.

'Number six. I'll rustle us up a spot of grub.' Brad pointed at the floor matting. 'No use in carrying on with this rubbish now.'

Grub as well! In her present belly-rumbling state it was a double temptation. No rushing unfed from school to gym like today. But what if she accepted and then went chicken again? The music was vital, but could she *listen* with him filling everywhere with his presence? The anxiety grew with the session and she admitted how she felt to Heather when they were getting ready to go home.

'Don't be an idiot,' Heather said.

'I'm not being an idiot, just realistic.'

'If you call realistic getting in a flap about something that hasn't happened and probably won't, then you're a bigger idiot than I thought. Why don't you tell him? He'll understand.'

70

'That I'm being a pig-headed twit...oh yeah!' Gail shoved the last of her kit into her bag and straightened up.

'I dunno what you're grumbling about. Stick with the fact that *you* are the one he's asked round.' There was a note of envy in Heather's voice. 'I'll expect a full report of everything mind.'

'We're only going to play a few records.'

'Oh yeah? Alone together...you want to watch it.'

'Don't talk daft. He's old enough to be me dad.' But being anybody's dad didn't seem his scene. Besides, how could she know? Tomorrow might produce a nagging wife and several rowdy brats. Then she remembered him saying: 'I'll rustle us up a spot of grub.' Not the remark of someone who went home to a ready prepared meal. He must be a loner. For some reason she couldn't explain she found herself hoping fervently this was so.

'The old 'uns are always the worst,' Heather went on darkly – and jumped when Brad's voice came over her shoulder.

'Hang on a minute will you?'

They turned as he turned back to Bob Penrose.

'Who does he mean, you or me?' Heather asked.

'You. Must be. He looked at you.' Gail was determined not to waste this chance. 'See you,' she muttered, and grabbing her bag escaped unobserved.

Outside darkness had been pushed back by the tall orange street lamps lining the pavements. Traffic had thinned but was still enough to keep Gail waiting impatiently on the kerb. A smell of diesel oil mingled with the sharp vinegary odour of fish and chips drifting from Mac's Fish Parlour down the street, sharpening her hunger. She was on the verge of abandoning everything in exchange for a bag of chips when the lights turned amber then red.

With an immense feeling of saintliness, Gail nipped round a Corporation bus, slid between a motorbike and a taxi, and ran hell for leather across the car park, under the

71

fly-over and round the back, arriving breathless on the doorstep of the Community Centre.

The interior was a mixture of aubergine carpet tiles, black plastic, off-white curtaining with a liberal scattering of scratched teak veneer. A lingering smell of school overlaid with coffee, cigarette smoke and the heavy perfume of a brightly blonde woman met her. The blonde woman smiled toothily.

'Through them doors, duck, down the corridor. Turn right. It's the room at the end.' She went back to pinning up a notice about the Christmas show rehearsals.

It was a music room. Going in Gail found not only the band in action, but an upright piano, two snare drums, a double bass propped in a corner and a flock of music stands huddled forlornly together against one wall.

Milton didn't see her. All his attention was on the music and the instrument he was playing. Not his guitar, she observed, but keyboard. Some kind of electric organ – Woolies variety. He was playing with an absorption she hadn't expected. Shoulders hunched, foot tapping – right inside the music. It added yet another dimension to this new Milton and brought back the feeling that she really didn't know him at all. The other three players were also strangers. She couldn't even remember their names, except for Jackson – looking for his musical washboard but not finding it. The drummer, a skinny youth in a striped bobble cap, was beating out an irresistible rhythm on bongoes wedged between his knees. It made her feet itch. The private jingle she had invented to concentrate her mind in the waiting periods at gymnastic meetings, matched the beat. She hummed it quietly, hugging the back of the room so she wouldn't be noticed.

'Malinova, Comaneci, Korbut and Kim
Malinova, Comaneci, Korbut and Kim Kim Kim...'

Tune and words fitted the rhythm glove-smooth and she

tried again, louder, getting so into it that she didn't see the drummer's moon smile, or his nod to the others letting them know they had an audience.

Milton didn't stop, but looked up and winked, continuing to play until the music rounded off with a running chord shared by keyboard and guitar. But long before that, Gail had dried up and was trying to look as if she had only been listening.

'Hey, sing over here why don't you?' Milton called, dashing her hopes. His unembarrassed pleasure at seeing her bubbled out in a stream of words: 'I'm dead pleased you've come. How long have you been here? Didn't see you come in. Didn't know you could sing either.'

'I don't sing I croak,' Gail lied firmly, to cut short any possibility of making an even bigger fool of herself. Moving nearer.

Milton slapped his knee and let out one of his rollicking laughs. 'If you keep your croaks to the beat it'll be okay — right fellers?' grinning at his mates and waving a large hand. 'This here's Clive... Gaz... Jackson – Gail.'

She said: 'Hi!' giving them a small embarrassed smile. 'I don't want to interrupt.'

'You aren't. We'd practically finished.'

'Can I listen in?' She had decided to keep the question about making a tape until Milton was on his own.

'Sure.'

She perched on the edge of the table, trying to ignore the glances flicked at her and then at Milton. They probably thought she was his girl. She had no way of knowing what stories he might have told them. Well, they could think what they liked. She didn't care.

It wasn't a long wait. The band played through the piece she had broken into; argued about a few bars; tried out two different variations of rhythm; listened to Milton's keyboard version; agreed on it, then began to pack up.

'Don't do anything I wouldn't, Milt!' Clive cuffed Milton's head as he passed him and closed an eye at Gail in a long slow wink.

Milton stretched out an arm, whisked off the bobble cap and chucked it through the doorway. 'Get knotted,' he said, grinning. Then to Gail: '*Now* tell me why you've come.' He had a habit of looking at her very intently and she wished that he would give it up. She couldn't think clearly and it was very important to be clear about the tape.

She slid off the table and wandered across to the piano, trailing her finger along the closed lid, trying to avoid his gaze. She explained about the Floor exercise, the need for new music, her feeling for Reggae, the problem of variation in rhythm.

'It 'ud be so difficult trying to do it just from records, even if I can find them,' she finished gloomily. 'I suppose...' she hesitated, suddenly shy about what she had come to ask.

He waited – silent.

She studied the floor tiles. 'You couldn't make a tape for me could you – with the group? Doesn't have to be proper, so long as it has the right feel.' She knew she hadn't explained concisely. Reggae was Reggae. You couldn't have some phoney version.

He didn't answer, but went to the piano, opened it and played a few chords; his right hand straying up the keyboard in a trickle of melancholy notes then back again; shifting to a foot-tapping tune.

'That's nice. It's Ragtime isn't it?'

He nodded and played a few more bars, lost the sequence, messed about trying to get it back, said: 'Oh nuts! Sorry,' and went back to the beginning. This time moving on into the music with gathering confidence.

She was no expert, but could see that he played with ease, hands moving over the keys as if they belonged there. The original brisk jogging tune melted into a slower more romantic passage which suggested various gymnastic moves. Scope for ballet steps, she thought. Pirouette; arabesque; a grand jeté there; then into flic-flac and tumbling. Yes! She felt excited. Inspired to try out some of the imagined moves, but there wasn't the space. She did experiment with a few dance steps, suiting them to the jog-trot passage Milton was playing.

'Like it?' he asked. 'Not Reggae, but I don't think that's on. Not the way you mean. Muck about with the rhythm and it would be like shifting the bottom tin out of one of them supermarket baked bean towers. Zowee...splat!' Both hands landed smack on the keyboard producing a jangle of sound. 'No go.'

They both laughed. Gail feeling easier with him than ever before. She liked him in an unbothered way, except when she remembered Heather's infatuation. Then she felt guilty, but tried to shake it off, not wanting to be tied in knots thinking about who fancied who and who was to be loser.

She asked: 'What's the name of that piece you were playing?'

'"Bethena". A bloke called Scott Joplin wrote it.'

'Oh him. Doesn't he write music for films?'

'A film.' Milton went back to playing. 'And he didn't write for it. His music got used. He's snuffed it.'

Snuffed it, seemed a favourite phrase, Gail thought, asking abruptly: 'D'you ever think about what it would be like to be dead?'

His hands hovered over the keys. He looked at her in surprise. 'Nothing to think. Dying – yes I think about that sometimes. Hope it won't hurt, that's all. But dead...' He slid into 'Bethena' again. 'I'll be just another bit of fertilizer helping to push up the daisies won't I.'

'You don't believe in Heaven and all that?'

He exchanged 'Bethena' for a hymn and she recognized 'All Things Bright And Beautiful'. Playing a final chord he closed the piano lid and picked up his guitar case. 'My sort of heaven would be right here and now. Have you got all night? If you have I'll describe it.'

She realized he was probably talking about how he thought the world ought to be organized, but reacted with a thrill before common sense came back. Romantic crap, she told herself, but couldn't quite blot out the wish that he might have been making a pass. She felt disturbed and rather silly – forever swinging one way and then the other – and wished she could straighten out her feelings.

Milton grinned. 'That's enough heavy stuff. Let's get a coffee.'

'Chips,' she said, responding with relief. 'We can eat them on the move. I can't spare time for coffee. Pat'll be doing her nut.'

They left the building. Gail amazed to find herself talking freely about the Council Home, the ever changing Housemothers, the other kids in care, her own lack of parents – ending with: 'But you know about that.' She wondered whatever had happened to her vow never to let outsiders into what was strictly private business.

'Tough,' he said.

She tensed again, but couldn't detect any pity.

He went on: 'I knew you weren't living with your parents, but not that you didn't have any.'

The street noises covered the silence, but a few yards further on he burst out: 'If it was me, I couldn't stand not knowing. Bad scene.'

'It is bad,' she said softly.

'Worse than knowing bad things about your mum and dad?'

He's asking because he cares, she said to herself fiercely. But the old rumbling confusions muddled her thoughts. Her cheeks burned. The fanning chill of air was a relief. Talk, she thought, that's all it ever is. And brooding. Never doing or learning or seeing for real. Just a load of

76

crappy brooding and talk. But did she want to know the truth after all? Mightn't it be so bad she couldn't bear it? Perhaps it might be worse to find out there was nothing to find. Just a dull story. A boring nobody of an unmarried mother who couldn't cope and had hopped it. No splendid African Princess in Kaftan and gold snake bracelets.

But nobody was Nobody.

'Well?' Milton persisted.

He was like Heather. Never gave up. She muttered: 'I'd rather know.'

'Then find out. There's ways. Birth certificates. Them down at the Welfare – they must know something. Kids don't sprout under gooseberry bushes. Isn't there someone you could ask?'

'You don't mean Mrs Bridgeman?' Gail was derisive.

'Who's she?'

'The social worker who keeps tabs on me. We have these interviews every now and again. Big deal.'

'Isn't there anyone you get on with better? Don't tell me it's illegal to go down and pick who you like. Or do you have to fill in a form?'

She said slowly. 'There's one person.'

'Who?'

'She's called Hilary something.'

'Hilary Something,' he made a surname of it. 'At least the Hilary bit isn't so unusual. Not like Cathie or Linda or *Something*!' A great gust of laughter blew out of him as he pushed open the door into Mac's Parlour.

Mouthwatering smells of fish and chips enveloped them.

'Stuff the research,' Gail said, hunger winning. 'I'll settle for a double portion with salt and vinegar.'

Milton launched another bellowing laugh. If I was to go out with him, Gail thought, meeting every eye in Mac's Parlour, I'd have to get used to this.

They bought chips, eating as they wandered up the street to the empty bus shelter.

Gail sighed as the last chip went down. 'Lovely!' She screwed up the greasy paper aiming for the litter bin, then licked her salty fingers. 'Now for trouble!' But she said it jauntily. Not looking forward to a session of Pat's fussy questions, but caring less. Milton, lolling against the glass wall of the shelter, had his hips thrust forward to help support the guitar case cradled in his arms. The rangy body was tightly sheathed in denim jeans. Her glance went on to his profile silhouetted against the glass, the planes of his face smoothly perfect under his magnificent bush of hair. Disturbingly perfect! She was caught off guard. If he asks me to go out with him now, she thought, I'll say yes.

But he didn't, and when the bus came, seemed to be deliberately avoiding anything except trivial chat. The latest chart topper. Recent movies Jimmy Lomas's terrible jokes. Her relief was underlined by disappointment.

When they got off, Milton hesitated.

Now, Gail thought, panic rising. He's going to ask me now!

'I dunno how exactly to say this,' he began awkwardly. 'Last time you weren't keen, but then tonight...well you seemed different somehow. Talking easy. And I thought, well I'll risk it I thought. Not wanting a flea in me ear like, but...' he broke off with a strangely reduced laugh. 'About your mum and dad. If you wanted a bit of moral support I'd like to help. We could go down the Welfare Saturday. Make a start.' His wandering glance suddenly focussed on her with the same intensity as it had in the music room. 'I know it's a real big thing for you.'

'Oh!' she said, shattered. A hysterical laugh rose in her throat. She fought it and lost.

Milton was hurt. 'What's so funny?'

But she could only shake her head, managing to stammer: 'I'll th...think it over.' The laughter hiccupped out. Irrepressible.

78

'Okay then, okay! See you.' Milton sounded huffy. He turned away and walked off up the road.

The laughter left with him. His hunched shoulders told her how he was feeling and she didn't blame him one bit. If there had been any way of putting things right she would have done it. There was no way.

Crossing the road she took the turning which led to the estate and the Home.

10

'Training for the hundred metre sprint last night were you?' Brad asked as he opened the door of the terraced house in Flaxhill Road. 'Come in, come in!'

Gail went into a narrow hall where a wallpaper jungle crawled up towards an elderly cream ceiling. Her imagination had painted his flat in clinical white and grey with Chinese matting, stripped pine furniture and a lot of cheerful scarlet cushions. She felt faint disappointment.

'Why didn't you stay on?' He led her into a dingy living room.

'I thought it was Heather you wanted to see.' She had been suffering all day from horrible unwanted jealousy because Heather had been picked for the Zone squad.

'I wanted to see you both, didn't she say?'

'She told me she'd been picked.' Gail recalled some other garbled words about Brad having asked if she'd gone, but they were thrown away in the middle of an excited stream of chat about her dad saying he'd give her lifts to Worle where the Zone squad trained, the new track suit she was going to get, Mrs Frost being somebody's cousin twice removed, and a whole heap more which Gail now couldn't remember.

Brad shrugged. 'It's of no account. I wanted to tell you together that you've both been selected.'

She couldn't take it in. Her knees began wobbling as if they had an independent life of their own, and she opened her eyes as wide as they would go, trying to get a clearer picture of his face so she could decide whether or not he

was having her on. The words would hardly come. 'Sh...
she... didn't say.'

'She didn't know.'

'But I ... but ... but when...'

He grasped what she was trying to ask. 'The day you
saw Mrs Frost at the club.'

'But I was terrible!'

'Not that terrible and she has a sharp eye for potential –
same as me,' he said dryly. 'The training sessions are once
a month, but you'll be starting in style with a trip to Lilleshall. She's got a weekend course planned for the
October break.'

Lilleshall. The National Sports Centre. Paradise!

'Think on. Sit yourself down and try a bit of this.' He
had taken a disc from the case under a small table where
the record player sat, and now put it on the turntable,
switching on, saying something like 'Artaters' before disappearing through the door.

Music swelled out and filled the small living room, covering up sounds of tea-making in the kitchen beyond. Hot
music. Somebody's jazz piano. What had he said? She had
only been half listening; head in the clouds and struggling
to take in his news. This piano stuff was clever, but she
didn't warm to it. Not like yesterday's Scott Joplin. If
Brad had none of his music on disc and 'Bethena' wasn't
in the record library, she'd really be in the cactus! Even if
Milton had been at school today, which he hadn't, there
was no way she could have asked him to make a tape for
her. Not after laughing like a drain last night. But now
they *must* make that tape – and quick!

She looked round the little room with a kind of awe.
Battered armchairs on worn floral carpet, unhelpful yellowish light issuing from under a lampshade that looked
like a leftover from a jumble sale, faded brown curtains,
drab fawn wallpaper – none of it mattered. The place was
a shrine. The badges pinned to one wall said so. The pen-

nants looped on blue ribbon said so. The wonderful post-
ers – of Nicolai Andrianov swinging over a pommel horse,
and her heroine Malinova poised high on a beam in front
of rows of blurred faces – proved it! From a gymnastic
nobody she had become if not a somebody, a nobody with
chances. Two hurdles leapt. She felt tall as a tree, and
scared to death in case this chunk of luck should disappear
as magically as it had arrived.

Elated though she was, the wall of gymnastic mementos
began to get through to her. She read the place names.
Denmark Sweden Roumania Spain East Germany Bul-
garia. Brad became even more of a mystery. She'd known
for weeks that he was a fanatic in the gym, but this International touch was new. How come a coach involved with
all these overseas matches was mouldering away as assis-
tant to old Penrose? It didn't make sense. Unless he'd
gone as a spectator. But that didn't make sense either.
Travelling took cash. This flat didn't talk lolly.

'Admiring my loot?' Brad came in with a tray and set it
down on the floor. 'You any good at making toast?' He
handed her a thick slice of bread and a toasting fork.

'Have you been to all them places?' she asked.

'Every one.'

In a flash it came to her that he must have gone as a
competitor. Yet she didn't recollect his name. She knew
most of the names of leading British gymnasts past and
present.

He was turning up the gas fire which had electric
magicoal logs in front. They flickered a revolving pattern
of orange mock flames over the navy blue of his track suit.
'Before the accident of course,' he added.

She almost dropped the bread she was spearing.

He knelt down, tranquilly taking the chipped teapot,
and poured tea into a mug, apparently unaware of having
said anything out of the ordinary. Gail saw milk in a bottle, sugar still in a paper packet, and felt obscurely

relieved that there was definitely no sign of a wife. With the relief came boldness.

'How long since your accident?'

He gave a short barking laugh. 'A year. Nearly sank my coaching career it did. Nearly sank me an' all! Car crash. Take sugar?'

'No.'

He smiled with the working half of his face. 'Good lass. In that case you're permitted a double ration of toast.'

She longed to ask what exactly had happened, if there had been anyone else involved in the crash, how long it took him to recover – but his shut-down expression discouraged questions. It was tantalizing. She drank some tea and turned the toast.

He had gone to draw the curtains when the piano music, with a series of crisp chords, came to an end. Two strides took him across the room. Removing the disc from the turntable he slotted it back into the sleeve. This like everything he did was thrusting; positive; allowing no room for indecision. If he was positive, she should be too, but instead was dithering.

'How d'you like Art Tatum?'

'He's okay.' She felt oppressed by having misheard the pianist's name. If she settled for Art Tatum before they had to go, it would be tidy and organized. Efficient. Brad would approve, and she wanted that approval. Wanted with all her heart to have this last knotty gymnastic problem resolved. The rest of her exercises were basically sound. The Floor alone remained a mess, she thought. If only she hadn't acted like a twit last night with all that hyena laughing, she'd be able to ask Milton to record 'Bethena' for her.

Brad, rummaging through the record case, said: 'Let's see what you make of our Oscar ... mind that toast!'

Smoke was rising. Gail pulled the bread from the fire and dropped it on a plate. The new music – lilting, catchy, varied – might have been specially designed for gymnastic moves. She listened to it flic-flac into slower balletic mood, then quicken again with runs and syncopated chords that were tailor-made for cartwheels and extended body-stretching shapes. But not mine, she thought, gloomily buttering the first piece of toast and offering it to him.

'Thanks.' He scrutinized her face. 'Not hooked?'

'I dunno...' She felt reduced by her inability to be neat and obliging. At this rate he would soon think she was being deliberately bloody-minded. But it was no use swopping one flop for another. Even if it was a lesser flop. Especially now the Individuals were possible, not a cob-web dream. 'Trouble is I'm hooked on the Scott Joplin thingy,' she admitted with a touch of desperation.

He bit the toast and chewed. 'In that case there's no more to be said. We'll try the record library.'

'I have.'

'Already?' There was admiration in his surprise.

'Dinner time.' She didn't mention the blast she had risked by breaking yet another school rule.

'And?'

'They haven't got it. I did ask.'

Brad slurped some tea, then put down his mug. 'This mate of yours, whatsisname...'

'Milton Pepper.'

'If I was to get permission for him and me to make a recording tape at your school, would he be willing? Is he good enough?'

'He's good enough,' she said quickly. 'But I dunno as he'd want to.'

Brad looked disbelieving. 'He's a performer isn't he? Plays with a band you said.'

She abandoned any attempt at trying to explain the delicate relationship between herself and Milton. It would sound wet. There was nothing else she could say.

'Well if he won't, I daresay one of the music staff might

if we get hold of a copy of the music.' He licked some escaped butter from his thumb, comfortably wedging his back against the chair, legs stretched out before the fire. Gail, also sitting on the floor and propped against the opposite hearthside chair, accepted this suggestion with relief. The fire's warmth, the toast and tea, relaxed and comforted her. From where she sat she could see the perfect elegance of Natasha Malinova, and *her* presence, even in flat photo form, put a seal on her content.

Brad followed her gaze. 'There's a dedicated lass. Gives her all twenty-five hours a day plus. Know what she does to prepare for competition?'

Gail shook her head.

'Two hours in her room the previous day, focussing her mind on what's to come – what she must do.' He tapped his forehead with a thick forefinger. 'Not just a question of endless physical slog. What goes on here is vital.'

'Is that what you think I should do?' she asked, stunned. Trying to imagine meditating with Lyn grizzling, and whoever else happened to be sharing the same bedroom doing their thing. Impossible!

'You could do worse than model yourself on Malinova where you can. Her life goes on oiled gymnastic wheels of course. Russia takes the sport seriously. 'Tisn't so easy in this country. A lot of blockheads looking on it as some kind of leisuretime play.' He sounded so ferocious she felt quite sorry for the blockheads. 'It can be,' he went on more mildly, 'but not if you're set on competing at International level.' The half smile came again. His hard straight look cutting into her with the sharpness of a knife. 'Frighten you?'

Frighten wasn't the right word. 'Depresses. It's all so hopeless with the school stuff and having to eat sarnies and dumplings when I'm trying to diet, and no cash for travelling, or not much, and not having enough training hours in the day with all the other things, and people who ought to be helpful not being.' The intensity of feeling took her to the brink of naming Penrose as an arch enemy, but respect for Brad's summary dealing with anyone who embroidered the truth held her back. She knew he was a stickler for exactness especially where truth was concerned, wearing it all like a hair shirt which rubbed against other people as well as himself. 'Impossibly hopeless,' she finished passionately.

'There's always hope,' he said with tacit understanding.

'Not for me there ain't.' She tumbled from the earlier heights into a pit of self-pity. 'Dunno why you bother with me.'

'Keep on in that mardy fashion and I won't be.' His voice was tart. Eyebrows meeting to make a deep furrow. 'As for why I am – there's good enough reasons.' Forbidding though his tone was, strong curiosity made her bold enough to risk an icy reaction.

'What reasons?'

He neither snapped, froze her, nor gave any answer, but seemed to disappear into private internal regions. Afraid she had gone too far, Gail nibbled toast, sipped tea, tried to swallow both silently and succeeded in sounding like a sludge-gulper. He didn't hear, or if he did made no sign; scowling at the fire. At the point where she began to think they would go on this way forever, he came out of himself as suddenly as he had vanished.

'You need a room of your own too if you are to do any good with the thought processes. I know you've not much chance of that. I've been in a Home myself. Dormitories we had. Six to a room. How many in yours?'

'Three.' She was staggered – another side of him she'd never guessed at. Was this why he'd taken particular interest in her? She wondered if he had no parents or the useless ones like weepy Lyn's.

He smiled. 'That's a step up I suppose, but we'll have to do something about finding you peace when you com-

86

pete on home ground. Easy enough when it's an away match. Just needs a word in the organizer's ear.'

She said tentatively: 'There is a single room at the Home. But a boy's got it.'

'Is he staying long?' Brad jumped on this possibility.

'I dunno. He might.' There was no telling how long anyone might or might not stay. Few stayed endlessly as she did.

'Hmm!' He was frowning again. Not at her but at the problem.

She was encouraged to ask: 'Were you in a Home long?'

'What? Oh, till I was five. After that I was adopted. Kind souls but I led 'em a dance. Teenagering wasn't my scene.'

'Perhaps they didn't understand you.'

He grinned at her slyly. 'I don't know. I might have been more co-operative if I'd known who I was. The Powers that Be didn't let you see your birth certificate in those days. And when all that changed I still had a battle.' He gave an abrupt incredulous laugh. 'There was this berk on one side of the table and me on the other. Between us, this file that was my life history. But could I see it? You'd have thought I was asking him to break the Official Secrets Act!'

'But he did show you?' she urged.

'Oh aye! In the end. And all a storm in a teacup it turned out.' He didn't offer to explain why and she didn't ask – another question quickening her heartbeats. She framed the sentence with care.

'If anyone wanted, especially that is, anyone who didn't know and wanted to find out, they could see their birth certificate could they? Just by asking?'

'I can't say. The law says yes, but there's still a deal of red tape. There always is. You'd need a sharp pair of scissors.' He glanced at his watch, seeming on the edge of saying more, but the promise not carried out.

'Should we be ready for off?' she asked, aware that the sheltering warmth and intimacy of the room was under attack. She wanted to go on and on sitting in front of the fire with him, talking. There was so much to dig up, share, ask.

'In a couple of minutes.'

Two sharp raps on the front door broke their privacy. She watched him go into the hall, annoyed by this intrusion and the fact that he didn't seem to mind it, but sparing a wry thought for Heather's remark about older men making passes at young girls. The joke had rebounded on herself. Nothing to do with passes after all, but sides. She and Brad together. Strangers definitely not wanted.

The stranger turned out to be an acquaintance. Hilary Something! The corners of Gail's mouth twitched up. Hilary smiled back brightly. Everything about her was bright. Hair, red leather jacket, white trousers. She knelt by the fire, holding out her hands.

'Cold?' Brad asked.

'Perished. I've been hanging around the Precinct waiting for someone who never came.'

'I'll get you some more tea. This lot's stewed.' He picked up the pot, heading for the kitchen. 'Mrs Clapton's giving us a lift, Gail. Might be worth trying her for that answer.'

'What's that cryptic remark supposed to mean?' Hilary asked as he disappeared. The hundred watt smile dimmed but didn't go out. She looked up with quick interest, and immediately Gail was conscious that the question had been intended for Brad alone, not as a casual inquiry to be flung at anybody. Conscious also that Hilary didn't come into the category of 'anybody'. The chance was there, too good to waste; too scouring to use.

'It wasn't anything much. We were talking about birth certificates.' The words rolled in her mouth like heavy unmanageable pebbles.

'Yours?'

'Well . . . partly.'

'And?'

Bright attentiveness glittered out, penetrating every shadowy corner. There was nowhere to hide. No place left to conceal anything and Gail felt trapped. She tried hard to be casual.

'Only wondering who looks after them . . . mine.' Her voice was aggravatingly husky.

'It'll be in your file in the office I expect. Or in the safe. You want to see it?'

'I wouldn't mind,' Gail said off-handedly, head on fire, blood pounding round her veins.

'I'll have a word with Mrs Bridgeman and let you know. Tomorrow.'

After years of dreaming, yearning, speculating, the simplicity of this arrangement stunned Gail. *In twenty-four hours she would know who she was!*

'I can't promise anything mind,' Hilary warned. 'There may be reasons why you might not be allowed to look. The Powers that Be are sometimes sticky if you are under eighteen. I don't mean to be crushing, but I just don't want you to be disappointed that's all. There may be no problems.'

Gail retreated into a front of indifference. 'It don't matter. It isn't that important.'

Hilary flicked at the curtains of hair, hooking them behind her ears. The colour in her cheeks had intensified. She lifted her chin. 'I'll use dynamite if I have to,' she said with such comic force that Gail felt a smile and had to let it go. Hope didn't come back, but Hilary's concern warmed her. She took another slice of bread and stuck it on the end of the toasting fork. You've got more urgent things to do than chase parents, she told herself, deciding instantly to brave it. Tomorrow she would see Milton and ask him to make that tape.

11

Nothing was resolved. The Powers that Be proved sticky. And Milton was absent from school for a fortnight.

"Flu,' Heather said knowledgeably as the car cruised through mild undulating Shropshire countryside.

They were being driven to Lilleshall by Heather's father in his smart yellow Datsun. Mr Stafford, a short stocky silent man, bald replica of his daughter with double the freckles, had a love for speed that didn't seem to go with his staid appearance. Absently Gail observed the sun on his nude skull raising a sheen like French polish.

'His mum told me,' Heather added.

'You went to see him?' Gail was jolted out of her preoccupation with the Floor exercise tape. She had until after the Lilleshall trip to come to a decision and felt pursued.

'Not exactly.' Heather turned round so that she could look directly into Gail's eyes. Her own, spaniel brown and doleful, appealed for sympathy. 'Mum and I took Gran down to the hospital yesterday for treatment and Milton's mum was on the clinic. I asked her.'

'But you don't know her.'

'Yes I do. Saw her with Milton in town once didn't I!'

There didn't seem to be anything to say to this, and Gail, slightly ashamed of being more bothered about the tape than Milton's health, withdrew from Heather's gaze and looked out at trees and hedge lines dashing by. There was a coppery hint of autumn in them; the green country beyond diced with rich brown fields ploughed for winter crops. She tried to keep her mind on what her eyes saw, not wanting to have to share Heather's love-lorn emotions.

She had enough problems of her own to cope with – in particular the recurring frustration of the interview with Mrs Bridgeman. The conversation went round in her head ...

'Sit down, dear. You've been asking to see your birth certificate I hear.'

'Yes.'

'Tell me, why do you want to see it now? In all our talks before you've never said.'

'I ... want to know about ... my parents.'

'Yes I realize that, but why now? I'm not asking out of nosiness, dear, don't think that, but as the person responsible for your welfare naturally I have to make sure it's in your best interest before letting you see such a confidential document.'

(Pause)

'I have got parents haven't I? Or did you find me under a gooseberry bush?'

'Now don't take that attitude, Gail. I have to be sure that I'm doing what's right. Believe me I have your happiness at heart. So give me straight answers and we'll sort this out in no time. No point in getting upset.'

'I'm not upset. I just want to know. Why won't you show it to me? It's only a bit of paper.'

(Pause)

'Look, Gail dear, it isn't just a simple matter like looking up a phone number in the directory. There are all sorts of things to take into account. All kinds of decisions to make. If you can't tell me why you want to see it now, then I can't make those decisions. Understand?'

'I just want to see it. Isn't that enough? *I want to*. They're *my* parents. Why shouldn't I see their names? Know who they were and what they did?'

'Because as I said before, unless you can satisfy me by explaining this sudden interest...'

'It's not sudden!'

'But it is! Have you ever asked me about this before?'

'No, but...'

'You may very well have had it in your mind, but then I'm not a mind-reader. I can only go on what I'm told. And all this trying to get in at the back door, not asking direct, not giving good reasons, makes me the tiniest bit suspicious, you see. As I was about to say, unless you can satisfy me by explaining this sudden interest I can't do anything but refuse. You must understand that I have a responsibility not only to you but to the Council – the people acting as your guardians till you are of age. We have to do what we consider is best for you. We'd be quite wrong to fill your mind with worries at this stage. Time enough for that. You've your school work to bother about, and with exams coming up so soon I'm sure that's more than enough for now. By the way, I hear you've taken up gymnastics again. Nice for you, dear. It's always good to have a hobby. You see, you are a very busy person. No good trying to squeeze in things that will only worry you.'

'But if you don't let me see, I *shall* worry.'

'And if I do, the worries will go away? I'm afraid you aren't seeing too clearly.'

'That's a laugh! If anyone is blind it's you...you old bag!'

'Gail!'

'That's what you are – an old bag full of win and words. You're mad because I didn't come and ask you first.'

'Nonsense. Insults will get you nowhere. You had better go away and think things over. Calm down. I have other things to attend to...'

'Oh...oh *shit*!'

(and the humiliating tears had come)

'She's ever so nice,' Heather said. 'Round and comfortable with a jolly smile.'

The distance from office to car seemed as far as Mars, and the atmosphere as foreign. Gail could hardly tell where she was, dizzy with the contrast of then and now. She asked: 'Who?'

'Milton's mum of course. Where were you?'

'Just thinking.'

'Didn't you hear any of what I said?'

'Yes...go on.'

'She said it had been a bad bout,' Heather continued. 'She couldn't say when Milton'll be back. D'you think we should send him a get-well card?'

The 'we' struck Gail as extremely ironic. If Heather knew how things stood between herself and Milton, she wouldn't be so sharing. In fact the whole situation was odd, considering Heather was so gone on him. On the other hand, how *did* things stand between herself and Milton? They weren't going out together. He hung around, but Heather had been there nearly every time. Only that conversation after the band practice had any significance – and the way he looked at her. But seen with miles and days between it all seemed flimsy. Make-believe.

'Well do you?' Heather persisted.

'If you like. Though we can't till we get back. We shan't be near any shops shall we?'

'I'd forgotten.' Heather's face clouded over, then brightened. 'Dad, you'll stop won't you...at the next newsagents or somewhere. We can get a card and write it. Then you can post it for us. *Please*!'

Mr Stafford made rumbling sounds of doubt.

'Oh go on, Dad. Look...over there's a place.'

The car had slowed down at a road junction. The street into which they turned was wide and only moderately busy.

'Just here, Dad!'

With a final rumble of objection, Mr Stafford drew into the kerb, stopped and felt for his cigarettes.

'Thanks, you're an angel.' Heather gave his cheek a fleeting kiss and scrambled out, looking in through the window at Gail. 'Come on!'

She got out, glad to escape the fuggy silent restraint of the car, following Heather across the street and into a shop where a selection of gaudy cards sat with elbows tucked in between a rack of sweets and another of newspapers and magazines. There wasn't much choice and they had to settle for a very white nightcapped man in a very red bed being ogled by an even whiter nurse. The caption read – 'And the best of everything' – inside – 'even getting well!'.

'It'll make him laugh,' Heather said.

Gail doubted it, but took the Biro and added her name. She felt remote, distanced by the thoughts in her head and they were back in the car and driving off again before she felt more normal; able to think about where they were going. Her spirits improved.

They were shooting along an uneventful road when Mr Stafford put on the brakes. 'There's the turning.' He swung into a winding avenue of tall trees. 'Private road.' For some reason this seemed to amuse him and he chuckled. 'Knew how to look after themselves!' He relapsed into his former silence and they drove on, slower now – the avenue opening out into rolling parkland, finally ending in a gravelled drive which led under a great arched gateway. There were buildings all round, some very recent, but the hub was a huge Gothic-grey mansion, castellated and ancient. Parking, they got out and took themselves and their luggage through a massive porch into a dark panelled hall where a stately baronial stairway wound up to lofty overhead floors.

'Wow!' Heather gazed round. 'Fancy having a pad of your own like this!'

Gail thought that it wouldn't suit her at all. It was much too strange and not at all homy, but she didn't say so.

The inquiry desk was tucked under the stairs. They booked in and the receptionist showed them the course programme pinned to a noticeboard.

'If you'd like to take your bags to your room, then come back down to the canteen, the evening meal should be almost ready,' she said. 'I'll try and find Mr Bradshaw for you and let him know you've arrived.'

They did as she instructed, saying goodbye to Mr Stafford, hardly noticing as he walked back to the car, lost in the excitement of being here. An excitement which kept Heather talking and Gail silent while they dumped their bags and found their way back to the hall.

The receptionist called to them: 'Mr Bradshaw's in the staff common-room. Just tap on that door there and go in.'

Feeling shy, almost overwhelmed, Gail let Heather lead the way. The staff common-room was panelled like the hall. High ceiling, heavy mantelpiece, deep bay window looking out over formal gardens – Gail took it all in. Three men and a woman were sitting in easy chairs. Brad was standing by the window. He nodded and came over.

'No trouble finding everything?' and before they could answer: 'The grub'll be ready in a couple of shakes. You'll be seeing the gyms after the meeting, but just come and take a look at this.' He led them through to another common-room which overlooked more of the gardens thick with trees and the parkland beyond. 'Get a feel of the place before you see the working parts. No comparison which is best for my money, but I reckon this isn't to be sneezed at.' He gazed out across lawns and flowerbeds, echoing Mr Stafford's remark: 'They knew what they were at.'

It was beautiful, Gail thought, but it wasn't what she really wanted to see. She was aching for a look at the gyms.

Brad became brisk. 'Right. Grub next. The canteen's this way. When you've had a bite to eat there's the meeting. You don't want to be late for that. Mrs Frost's hot on punctuality.'

He was right. When they got to the lecture room, Mrs Frost was already there.

'Heather, Gail...come in and find a seat.' She smiled at them and Gail thought she looked – if it was possible – neater and more smart in her deep red track suit than she had in the flowing dress. The ash-blonde hair lay close to her head, perfectly trained. Everything about her was well disciplined. Her bright restless eyes took in each member of the Zone squad as they hurried in. 'That chair there...bring it over...that's right.' And as everyone settled: 'I'm really glad there aren't any missing faces. It's going to be a splendid weekend...splendid. Hard work. Slogging till you drop and then getting up and slogging some more. But I know you all love hard work!' A ripple of laughter met her and her smile grew. 'Now...your timetable. There's a copy for each of you. If you wouldn't mind passing them round please. I'll go through it with you and explain.'

Gail glanced down the list. Saturday was crammed to bursting. Warm-ups, group and individual training sessions, a ballet class, a special physical conditioning period...

'When you'll train for increase of strength – most important,' Mrs Frost said, 'as is the clinic when we shall analyse each of your routines and your progress...'

And after an evening meal, time set aside for watching films of various championship performances.

'If we can keep awake,' Heather muttered in Gail's ear.

Sunday morning was to be given over to the official World Set routines. The afternoon to dance and choreography. After a debriefing meeting and tea they would be free to go home.

'A tightly packed weekend,' Mrs Frost concluded. 'I want you to put every last ounce of yourselves into each section of the course. Don't waste a single minute. This is a marvellous opportunity for really improving your stamina and performance!' She had a punchy way of speaking. Enthusiasm seemed to bubble out of her voice, her smile, her direct sparkling gaze. It reached out to Gail, heightening the excitement she already felt.

They left the lecture room and were taken across to the newest gymnasium.

'It isn't the only one, you understand,' Mrs Frost said, hand on the door. 'The old indoor stables have been converted for use as well, and there's the main hall. But this is special.'

It was. Gail felt as if she had walked into a Science Fiction film set. A huge prefabricated tunnel structure, made from some thick plastic material the colour of clotted cream, was stretched over a metal framework. But most stunning of all was not the gymnasium lid, but its floor. The major part was filled with a deep T-shaped pit stuffed to the brim with chunks and strips of plastic foam. A rainbow of multi-shaped off-cuts in a frame of deep blue matting.

'Two metres,' Mrs Frost said, when Gail asked how deep.

Two metres would be over her head. She would disappear beneath a mountain of foam never to be seen again!

Mrs Frost's enthusiasm spilled over. 'Splendid isn't it? Based on the Russian gyms. The pit has a special system of air ducts at the bottom and sides to prevent a build up of condensation.' She looked approvingly along the pit's length. Gail, at her shoulder, saw high bar, rings, asymmetrics, second bar and beam straddling it in a line. The vaulting horse rested to the left, foam beyond; pommel horse nearer the entrance. Warm air blowing in from big angular pipes provided a tropical heat. It was fantasy. Something beyond dreams. She felt breathless and staring as if she had been lifted up and placed in another world that was outside any she knew.

'Like it?' Brad asked.

She nodded, speechless.

'A bit different eh?'

She nodded again.

'How weird can you get?' Heather whispered. 'No mattresses, just a ruddy great heap of bath sponges.'

One of the unknowns, a large girl with country-red cheeks and tight yellow curls, heard and giggled. 'Know where to come when we need one then, don't we!' She pushed a determined toe into the nearest spongy strip.

'We'll be in here first thing tomorrow after the warm-up,' Mrs Frost said, holding open the door for them to file through, and continuing the tour.

In a different way Gail was as bowled over by the secondary gym. That anyone had been rich enough to provide not just stables, but this vast indoor area where horses could be tended and exercised in bad weather, was hard to grasp.

'Lucky horses,' she said to Heather that night when they were in their neat bedroom in the hostel block. The curtains were drawn; the overhead light switched off. Between them on a table was a bedside lamp, low-key and intimate.

'Horses?' Heather sitting up in bed was filing her nails with an emery board.

Gail stretched out luxuriously, putting her arms behind her pillowed head. 'Yes. In the old days when this place was the Duke of Whatsit's hunting lodge. Two visits a year and a mile of horses to keep him and his mates happy. I should think they must've had a mile of servants as well to run a place like this.'

'No problem in those days. He'd got the cash.' Heather began to press down her cuticles using the end of the emery board. Gail watched her. She looked plump and pretty with her hair loose over her shoulders. Gail wondered if Milton fancied girls who were plump and pretty –

like marshmallows. What did Milton see as 'his type'? It wasn't something she had considered before.

Heather sighed. 'Great to have all that lolly.'

'Would you like to be rich?' Gail asked.

'Yes. Wouldn't you?'

'I suppose so.'

'You don't sound too sure. Think of being able to buy clothes and shoes and go out for meals and see films and fly off to the Bahamas just whenever you wanted.'

'That would be great.' She knew she still didn't sound enthusiastic.

Heather looked up from her nails. 'I never knew anyone like you before. You're so . . . different.'

'What's different about me?' It was a daft question. What wasn't different about her!

'I dunno . . . sort of super-cautious. As if you're afraid to let out what you really think and feel in case someone kicks you where it hurts.' Heather gave her a candid smile. 'You don't mind me saying that do you? I wouldn't be so blunt only I feel we know each other pretty well now. I mean what's a friend if you can't speak straight from the shoulder?'

The warmth spreading through Gail's body had nothing to do with the covering of bedclothes. In all the rooms shared throughout her life, none before had been with a self-confessed friend. She felt deeply touched, and said gruffly: 'That's okay,' the sensation of doors opening to her, very strong.

Heather slotted the emery board back into her make-up bag and slid down in her bed. 'I'm glad you don't mind. I've been wanting to say that for ages, but didn't like to in case you took it the wrong way.' She switched out the light.

Darkness closed round them. Lying on her back with eyes wide open, Gail saw light filtering through the curtains and stippling a pattern of dots and stripes across the ceiling. From a distance came tranny music, an owl calling, and nearer, feet crunching over gravel below. As each switched off – deep silence. It had been a long extraordinary mind-blowing day, but she didn't feel sleepy.

Neither did Heather. 'I'm glad you got picked for the Zone squad. If it had been me and not you I'd have felt bad.'

Gail said nothing, recognizing that in the reverse circumstances, except for brief feelings of sympathy, she wouldn't have been particularly concerned. She felt faintly guilty.

Heather didn't notice the silence. 'When you didn't come to the club all that time, it wasn't half such fun. Nobody to talk to.'

'What about Cathy?' Gail asked, thinking that they went to train not chat, but pleased all the same.

'She's okay, but you can't talk to her. Not seriously. Gymnastics is just a hobby with her.'

'Nice hobby for you, dear...' Mrs Bridgeman's comment came back underlining what Heather meant. With a buoyant sense of release, Gail knew they were on the same wavelength. No need to tell each other that gymnastics had to be a passion – *was* a passion. The tight pocket of ambition she carried around day and night, opened out. With the darkness as a boost, she found the nerve to ask:

'If you had to choose between being a gymnast and something else that mattered very much, which would you pick?'

There was a long pause before Heather said slowly: 'I don't know.'

With a slight sense of shock, Gail said: 'The something else must be pretty big then.'

'It is.'

'What is it?'

Another extended pause, then:

'Milton.'

The air between them seemed to turn brittle. From simple awkwardness, the triangle with Milton at the apex became infinitely more complicated and serious. And yet it was ridiculous, Gail thought. Milton was nobody's boyfriend. He'd said nothing, done nothing.

'You must think I'm crazy.' Heather's voice came muffled as if she was partly·under the bedclothes.

'No...yes...no...' She couldn't sort out what she thought except that by not mentioning the visit to Milton's band practice, or admitting she too found him attractive, she wasn't being a friend in Heather's terms. She badly wanted to be that friend, but how could you say 'I fancy him too' and not twist the friendship into a competition or kill it stone dead? Besides, she wasn't sure how she felt any more. The urgency had transferred from fancying Milton to everything here. Instead of dreaming about him leaning against the bus shelter, or the way he had looked at her, or the thrill of being close to him, all her thoughts now centred on that fantastic gym. She had only to imagine being in it tomorrow – pounding into a vault; swinging high over the asymmetrics and that incredible spongy pit; sweating and striving for perfection – to feel a greater thrill of expectation. By comparison Milton seemed unimportant. Or did he? She couldn't decide and turned over in bed, the turmoil turning with her.

'I can't stop thinking about him.' Heather's voice sounded as if she had blankets crammed into her mouth. 'All the time. He gets between me and essays. Even when I'm training I'm only three quarters there. The other quarter of me wondering about him, about his family, about things he does. Playing soccer. Swimming. I bet he looks gorgeous in swimming trunks and nothing else. His skin's like black silk.' She groaned. 'Oh...I'm obsessed! D'you think he likes kippers for breakfast? I love kippers.'

In Gail's sensitive frame of mind, the contrast of black

101

silk and kippers proved too much. She burst into helpless laughter, aware that it was ill-timed but unable to do anything to stop it. Tears trickled over her cheeks. Her ribs ached till she had to curl up to ease them. When she finally managed to control herself there were other sounds in the room. In the dim night light she looked over the dividing bedside-table.

Buried in pillow, Heather was crying.

For a few seconds Gail lay still, filled with dismay and not knowing what to do. The precious enjoyable ease of only five minutes before was demolished. She swore softly. Then, as the sniffling sobs went on, slid out of bed and knelt on the carpet tiles, putting out an awkward hand to stroke the tousle of hair.

'What's wrong? Is it me? I didn't mean...'

Heather's shoulders twitched. With a choking snort she wrapped the pillow over her ears, rocking from side to side.

Gail was alarmed. Surely just laughing couldn't cause this distress? She didn't know what to say or do, helpless in the face of such misery. Heather sobbed on, and in desperation she put an arm round the shaking shoulders.

'Heather, love, what is it? Don't cry...'

From her buried position Heather suddenly turned and flung her arms round Gail, pulling her close, words bursting out of her like hiccups:

'It's... Milton... he doesn't... hasn't... oh... nobody understands... Mum says...' The crying took over again and Gail, appalled, didn't learn what it was Mum had said. Years of carefully built self-protective barriers were hacked away. She felt completely shaken. Aiming a kiss at Heather she landed on an exposed ear tip, bumping her nose. The strength of Heather's commitment to Milton came walloping home. But on the heels of this revelation was a cool amazement that anyone could be so infatuated. She's acting like she's been jilted or widowed or something, Gail thought, and wondered at herself for being so moved yet feeling scorn at the same time. With sharp clarity she realized that the time for sharing her own feelings about Milton, however uncertain, was over. With it, any hope of securing the bond of friendship with Heather.

The sobs subsided and Heather unwound her arms, ferreting after a handkerchief. 'You must think I'm raving.'

Gail sensed that the atmosphere had sharpened. 'My fault for laughing.'

Heather found her handkerchief and blew hard. 'No it's not. It's me. Time of the month. I came on today just before we left home would you believe! It always makes me touchy as hell. I snap at everybody and end up bawling. Like now. I'll be okay tomorrow.' Her words rattled out like dried peas, and she laughed – a tremulous watery unconvincing sound which said that the exposed moment was almost over.

Gail got up, stumbling back into bed. All warmth gone, she pulled the bedclothes tight under her chin as if in defence against cold and further revelations. The sweet taste of everything had turned sour. This was what happened when feelings got the upper hand. Holding back, being cautious, was right. Heather could say what she liked.

'But all the same I'm not sorry that you know,' Heather said. 'It's such a relief knowing that somebody who understands knows. If it never comes to anything, at least I'll know you know, and you'll know I know you know and understand . . . if you get my meaning. What I'm trying to say,' she concluded, 'is that *I'll* know and *you'll* know.'

More than you'll guess, Gail thought, not sure whether she wanted to laugh at the garble or cry with disappointment, or merely blot out everything by going to sleep. She wondered if the episode would colour the rest of the weekend.

It did. But not quite as she expected.

12

They got up to a shining day with a set of starlings racketting on a nearby roof, the chorus joined by an occasional soft-spoken pigeon. The previous night wasn't mentioned though the knowledge of it hung in the air. To Gail's relief the conversation, if chirpy and surface, came easily enough. They fooled about. Chucking towels. Giggling. Heather doing a princely imitation of Penrose calling the class to order – a pinch of the nose, shoulders up and down – all so accurate, Gail was left doubled up on her bed. Between gasps her hopes for the weekend improved...if only she could give Mrs Frost a four star taste of her work. The Floor exercise weighed heavy.

'What'll you do about it?' Heather wanted to know as they collected scrambled eggs, toast and boiling tea, going to sit with the others.

'Nothing till I get back. Providing Mrs F don't kick up a fuss.'

'Haven't you any ideas?'

Gail recognized the onset of a persistent question session. She felt her diaphragm tighten. This was the moment to drop a word or two about her plans for Milton to make a tape, but after last night there seemed too many hazards. 'I know what I want. Reggae. But it isn't suitable Brad says. There's a Scott Joplin piece though.'

'Which?'

'"Bethena".'

'Never heard of it. Where did you come across that?'

Gail cut off a large slice of toast, piled it with egg and crammed it in her mouth. Meryl, the large girl with the blonde bubble cut and country-red cheeks helped the delaying tactics by choosing that moment to lean across the table and ask for the marmalade. Gail gave the pot a shove.

'Thanks.' Meryl scooped some out with her knife then used it to point. 'See who's here?'

Swivelling in her chair, Gail saw Mrs Frost and Brad inside the doorway talking to a bearded man in a blue track suit with a white trim.

'Who's he?'

Meryl looked surprised. 'Don't you come from Coventry?'

'Yes.'

'Then I'd have thought you'd know. He runs the Centre of Excellence there. He's a National coach. *The* National coach.'

Gail put down her fork, appetite reduced by a burst of adrenalin. Of course she knew – in theory. Not in practice. Jackie had talked endlessly about the once-a-month weekend scheme for training up-and-coming gymnasts in the same college gym where the Elite group worked. Had filled the air with tempting hints – 'One day; perhaps; maybe; if you work hard...'

Nothing had happened. Now the man who masterminded it was here. Flesh and blood.

'He's come to give us the once-over,' Meryl said.

'Pass the butter will you?' Heather asked and took a yellow nut with a lack of fluster which impressed Gail. 'Who told you?'

'Mrs F.' Meryl equally undisturbed, made a whirlpool with teaspoon and tea.

'D'you mean he's come to coach *us*?' Gail asked, with a new hope springing up. Her mind took off...she was picked for the National squad, International matches ...was travelling – Hungary Sweden America. All in an instant. And in another instant was back in the canteen

105

with the remains of toast and egg on her plate, hopes in the gutter.

'No he hasn't. But he keeps his eyes open.' Meryl was watching her, and with cover-up haste Gail seized her cup, took a careless scalding gulp and spat tea over plate and table.

'Christ!'

'He's that important!' Meryl said, and grinned.

The blister turned out a mixed blessing. Nagged by her sore mouth, Gail threw herself into the run-around skip jump warm-up and suppling exercises in the old stables with extra gusto.

'Did you see the approving looks Mrs F was giving you?' Heather asked as they walked to the Science Fiction gym (nicknamed the Foam Dome) for apparatus work.

'And you. And everybody.' Gail was deliberately off-hand, seething with hope inside. If only she could keep it up.

In the gym she was selected to vault.

'Let's have a look at the long arm overthrow you've been working on,' Mrs Frost said.

Gail turned to pace the distance for her run-up and saw the door open. Three people came in. A large man in an out-of-place lounge suit, and two others, track-suited. One was the National coach. He looked straight at her. Past her. Scanning the gym before skirting the pit where he squatted down, observing a thin boyish girl Gail knew as Stella, perform a stream of tumbling along the matting strip.

Gail faced the horse. Watching eyes seemed everywhere, feeding her burning inner need to do well. Brad glowering; Meryl (who winked); Heather; Mrs F waiting; Stella walking back along the matting. Everyone it seemed, except *Him*! Aware that her concentration was being divided, she tried to channel mind and vision on the Reuther board, vaulting horse, foam bed beyond. Stroking her thighs with nervous fingertips. Flexing up on her toes. Almost single-minded. But distracted again as she began the sprint by a streak of wonder about the spongy waiting unknown. Would she drown? Suffocate? Eyes nose ears spongily blocked? What the hell – it was soft wasn't it?

She came down on the Reuther board fractionally too soon. Knew it. Felt the angle of flight to be wrong. Smacked on to the leather out of place and toppled over unceremoniously into the warm soft foam that stroked and bounced her back with little puffs of tepid air.

The eyes were there as she surfaced, head and shoulders above ground. Same eyes, plus. *He* had swivelled round. Now he got up.

'You didn't get your legs quickly enough to the vertical line in the first flight,' Mrs F said. 'Try to keep a very tight body position. In with that tummy. Have another go.'

Gail clambered out, cursing under her breath, and paced the run-up distance again.

The National coach moved as she moved, she noticed, coming to rest where he could have a midway side view of her sprint. Brad was with him.

This time she hammered her concentration into shape with fierce determination. Ran at the board. Pounded. Felt her heels lift quickly back and up, but somehow lost the usual spatial awareness of where she hung in the air. A feeling of inaccuracy with her all the way. Over. Under. Surfacing. Out ... and face to face with *Him*.

'You want to watch that third stride, Sunshine. Each time you hesitate. Because of that you get your timing wrong, come down on the board wrong, hit the horse wrong. Spells disaster! Again.' The short beard went up and down in command. The slightly prominent eyes implacably observing as she paced back to the beginning.

She saw Brad's face frowning disapproval. He didn't speak, but in her ears were his words so often heard. 'Shovel out all that everyday crap in your mind about laddering your best tights this morning and who'll be holding your hand in the back row of the pictures tonight. Take your time. Focus!'

Mental blinkers on, staring at the blueness between her feet, she focussed. And when control was complete began the run-up, thinking only of her body and where it was going. This time each stride was unhesitating. She hit the Reuther board, driving from it, knowing at every split second exactly where she was as she came into and struck strongly from the horse. A clean twist and she was over, falling down down into the pit.

'Splendid! Keep that up and you'll make a nine eight in the Apparatus Championships I shouldn't wonder.' Mrs Frost's smile was full blown, but better still was Brad's short nod of approval.

So she knows, Gail thought, looking round for other praise. But back turned, the National coach was watching Heather cartwheel into a dismount off the beam. A particularly tricky movement that she performed with finesse and only a slight loss of balance.

'Good enough for perfect I'd say,' Gail consoled her as they pulled on their track suits at the lunch break.

'Not what *He* said.' Heather jammed her foot into a training shoe and bent to lace it.

'Brad?'

'No.' She pointed at the figure of the National coach at the far end of the gym. '*Him*!'

'Tell me.'

'That I'd ruined a passable performance with the flabby finish of a toad who's been at the vodka all night.' Heather unwound, jammed on the second shoe and groaned. 'I don't know why we do it. I really don't. We must be mad!'

'Crackers,' Gail agreed.

'Know something? When we were talking last night, you never said what your choice 'ud be.'

Gail was startled, having thought Heather would never mention last night again. 'Oh gymnastics. I'm a sucker for punishment.' It was an unthinking reply, surprised out of her. With a sense of wonder she realized it was the truth. Without a shadow of doubt the Who-am-I hunt had radically changed. It was difficult to pinpoint what the difference was, but she knew that finding out who her parents might have been, or even if they still existed, had slipped behind.

Heather laughed. 'You always were.'

'Now what d'you mean this time?'

'Taking everything to heart. You're so serious.'

Gail was startled a second time, never having imagined herself as being particularly serious. If anyone was serious it was Heather with her mooning over Milton.

Heather laughed again. 'Just joking.'

In Gail's experience jokes had as a rule a core of truth. At the door she stopped and looked back at the glowing pearly walls, the rainbow pit, the line of apparatus steely and strong. This was serious if anything was. It demanded everything – every moment, every thought, every ounce of strength – with ruthless totality. Another world altogether from the Home and school and work or dole queue, whichever. Was it her world? Had she the guts for it? Was she *serious* enough to give the whole of herself to it? In the past she'd thought so, but knew now how shallow her knowledge had been of the devotion demanded. Narrow yet curiously big was this gymnastic world. Full of serpentine temptations of success, with all the bewitching trappings of travel, mingling with the greats, even being famous. What if she was to see herself in the newspaper? A big glamorous photograph of herself alone...in a National daily...

'I wondered where you'd got to.' Heather reappeared

109

through the doorway. 'I'd got right to the path talking to myself about next weekend. Felt a king-sized nana when I realized you weren't there. Are you coming?'

Gail picked up her training bag. 'What's about next weekend.'

'My birthday party. Gran's going back home this week, so the fun's on. I hope Milton's well enough to come.'

Half in, half out, Gail glanced back down the gym. At the far end *He* was talking to Stella. She felt a pang of jealousy and frustration, tried to analyse it and couldn't. Not until she had walked with Heather to the canteen door did she realize that her usual reaction to birthday chat wasn't there. It had been such a big issue for so long, and now it had gone. The card she had bought for sending to herself wouldn't be needed after all.

'You look as if somebody's told you the world is on fire,' Heather said.

'Don't talk so daft.' How could you explain something like that? Gail pushed through the swing doors and went into the humming canteen trying to decide what food would be least painful to her mouth. She was so *hungry*!

13

The side street where Milton lived was Edwardian terraced with a corner shop jammed full of tinned food and
sweet jars — doormats, mops and vegetables outside — the
pavement kerb edged by a broken line of cars. In front of
Milton's house was a Yamaha motorbike which reflected
the last rays of chilly winter sun from gleaming chromium.
The short garden path patterned with red and cream
diamond tiles led to a freshly painted red door with a new
brassy knocker shaped like a Grecian urn. Everywhere
looked impressively spick and span. Almost discouragingly
neat. Gail was in half a mind to turn round and go away,
but didn't. Lifting the knocker. Rapping.

Milton opened the door, letting out strains of music,
delicious smells of cooking and a burst of laughter. He
said: 'Gail!' softening his amazement with the size of his
smile.

'Thought I'd find out how you were as you didn't turn
up at school today.' He was thinner than ever. Baggy
jersey drooping from bony shoulders. She glanced back
down the path asking: 'That your dad's motorbike?'

'Our kid's . . . me brother Errol's.' He looked at it with
as much pride as if it had been his own. 'He's mad on
Yams.'

'D'you ride it?'

'Only pillion. I *can* ride if that's what you mean, but . . .'
He laughed, turning down his thumbs.

'The cops 'ud nick you, or you'd crash?'

'What is this, some kind of quiz?'

She felt rather silly. Her questions had come out of the

awkwardness of not quite knowing how to handle the situation.

'Heather told me you had flu,' she said abruptly.

'Did she?' He seemed surprised. 'I'm okay now. Fit as a flea,' thumping his chest with an uncomfortable laugh, giving her the odd impression that being ill was an embarrassment to him. 'I'd've been back today but our Jannie was sick and somebody had to stay in with her.'

'She your sister?'

'Yeah.'

The warmth of the hall was coming towards her in waves. It looked cosy inside. A place where you would want to be. She felt constricted – unable to say outright the real reason for her visit; skirting round it.

'Heather'll be pleased you're better. She wouldn't want you to miss her party.'

'Oh that!' He didn't seem enthusiastic. 'When is it?'

'Saturday.'

'You going?'

'Yes.'

'Guess I will too then,' laughing again, making a joke of it.

Her discomfort grew. 'I can't stop long. I've got to get back for me tea and then there's the club.'

'But you will come in for a minute? Have a cup of something. I want to hear about how you got on at that place.'

'Lilleshall? It was great.' She went into the narrow brightly lit hall, unavoidably brushing against him as she passed. She had forgotten how his physical presence affected her. The size of the hall forced them to touch again as he shut the door, buzzing her flesh.

He said: 'Go in the kitchen,' pointing to a door ajar at the end of the passage. 'There's somebody I'd like you to meet.'

She was immediately resistant. She hadn't come for a social visit. This chance she'd made – which had cost her

112

a good deal in courage, coming to a house where she'd never been before – was being threatened. She said hastily:

'Hang on. I want to ask you something first. About the music.'

He looked surprised, but took her into the front room. 'More peaceful.'

Except for a Western raging across the colour telly, it was. Milton switched it off. With half of her attention Gail noted green wall to wall carpet, poppies blooming on fresh wallpaper, well-polished piano, yellow dralon three piece suite – on the sofa of which a small girl lay asleep covered with a checked travelling rug. An electric fire gave out a pleasant homely warmth.

'Don't mind our Jannie,' Milton said. 'She won't wake. And she hasn't got anything catching. Just something she ate yesterday. Now – what music.' He sat down suddenly in a chair, holding on to the arms.

'You okay?' Gail asked, alarmed. He looked very tired.

'Yes ... yes.' He sounded testy, but put things right with his smile. 'Knees on strike that's all. Being in bed twenty-five hours a day 'ud flatten a dinosaur. Go on.'

She perched on the edge of the chair opposite and told him about the Floor exercise still being a flop; that she had settled for the Scott Joplin but couldn't get hold of a recording; that the Apparatus Championships were getting hairily close and that she had to be able to tell Brad what she intended to do that night or all hell would bust loose.

'I haven't got "Bethena" on disc or tape,' he said.

'But you can play it. We could make a recording couldn't we?'

'Depends how soon. Jackson's got the recording gear. I'd have to get in touch. Might be able to get hold of it for the day after.'

'That's fine but...' She explained that the recording

113

had to be specially arranged to fit in with her moves.

'Which you've got worked out,' Milton said.

'Not exactly. They need to be done with you there and my coach. So we can decide just where to slow the music down or quicken it up...together.' She liked that thought and looked at him hopefully. 'How about recording it at school tomorrow? On the piano in the hall. Room for all three of us.'

'If Jannie's okay I will.'

There always seems to be some obstacle, she thought, wondering with despair if her Floor exercise was destined to be a flop for ever and ever. She clamped her teeth together, unconsciously making her jaw jut. Just let him or anyone try and muck it up!

Milton grinned. 'It won't I promise.'

'What won't what?'

'All hell bust loose. I'll make sure of being at school the day after, even if I don't make it tomorrow. Now come and meet the old dear.'

'Your mum?' As Gail got up Jannie stirred in her sleep but didn't wake.

'Her too, but I really meant the other.' Milton chose to be deliberately mysterious.

They went into a tropical kitchen where Mrs Pepper, a waterproof apron swathing her stout body and generous smears of flour along her bare arms, was rolling pastry at a table. On the other side, with a cup of tea in front of her, sat an old woman whose silver hair sparkled tinselly under the strip light.

'Gail, this is me Mum. And this is Mrs Box... remember?'

He's got a nerve, Gail thought, immediately alert and wary as she took in the brown eyes, rosy cheeks, skin net-worked with wrinkles, hearing aid. There were hellos and smiles and well-I-nevers and cheeriness and radio pop to battle with besides her inner turmoil.

114

Mrs Box stretched out a hand, and after a hesitation, Gail took it. The bulk and strength of grip was remarkable. Out of keeping with old age. There was nothing frail about her – a large-boned stocky old woman.

'Your name's Knight, isn't it love?' A crooked warming very young smile.

Gail smiled back, enough to be polite, and took away her hand. 'Yes.' She couldn't blame Milton for setting up this meeting. He hadn't known she would call in on the way back from school.

'Fancy that!' Mrs Box's Birmingham voice sounded genuinely delighted. 'I used to know some people called Knight. In fact my brother Vic married a girl by that name. Bella Knight. Small world isn't it?'

'Milton said.'

'Did he say as it was me as introduced them?' Mrs Box didn't wait for any reply. 'She was ever such a nice girl. A real friend. I knew her first yo see. We worked in the same munitions factory. This was right back in the First World War, before I got to be a nurse. Such a long time, yet it's like yesterday thinking about it. They say the years do that when yo gets to be old. Second childhood!' She laughed, and Gail remembered Milton's comment about needing a spare week for chats with Mrs Box. She didn't have a spare week now, only half an hour or so before the evening's round of homework, tea and training, but couldn't bring herself to break away.

She said diffidently: 'Bella wouldn't be a Knight then, not when she got married.'

'No, love. Palmer. That was my name too of course, before *I* got married. They didn't have any kiddies either. Real shame that was. Made Bella real sad. Her and me used to talk about it sometimes, both being in the same boat. "A home's not a home without children" she used to say.' Mrs Box sighed, then laughed at herself. 'Hark at me! Getting as sentimental and soft as old soap!'

'Did she...' Gail had difficulty in forming the words, 'have any brothers or sisters?'

'Two brothers. Jack got killed out in France, but there was Luke her twin. Strange boy he was, but yo couldn't say he wasn't brave. He was a conchie in the days when it wasn't fashionable. They gave him a rough time in the war, but he was a survivor – tough as old boots.'

It was more than enough for now. Gail watched Mrs Pepper's floury capable hands rolling the pastry strip. The worst part of listening and letting yourself be drawn in, she decided, was managing the hopeful feelings. They got smashed so easily. There was nothing in the world to connect her with these dead and vanished Knights except the colour of her skin. She thought of the discovery at Lilleshall that gymnastics came first, and wondered how she could be so changeable. It was an endless tug-o'-war. She looked up at Milton.

'I ought to be going or I'll be late for the club,' and to Mrs Box: 'It's been nice meeting you.' She found that she meant it.

'And yo, love. If yo fancy another chat when yo aren't in a rush I live only a stone's throw from here. Bottom of the street. Milton'll show yo. I do like a chat about the old days. I can tell yo all about Bella's old grandad – the Admiral they used to call him.' She laughed. 'There I go... talking! Yo just have to say "Shut up, Emily" when yo've had enough or I'm likely to chew your ears till they drop off!' The crooked warming smile came again and seemed to rub out the years so Gail could guess at how she must have looked as a young woman. She would never have been pretty, but it would have been a face to remember.

'I meant what I said. On my own nowadays, so it's always a treat to have visitors. Don't get out so much as I used.' Her laugh was as sturdy and individual as her smile.

Gail felt a touch of pity. Someone else without people. Was it more lonely to have had relations and lost them, or to do without always? She had no answer.

'Don't forget now,' Emily said.

'I won't,' Gail replied; to get away not because she intended visiting.

Mrs Pepper stuck the last clove into the last apple, folding round the overcoat of pastry, then pushed the full tray into the oven, snapping shut the door. She was sweating freely, but when Milton suggested opening the window reacted with swift overdone anxiety.

'Never mind that. I don't want you in bed again. And don't you catch your death in that cold doorway,' as he went down the hall with Gail.

He opened his eyes wide, not answering, but sharing his reaction with her by means of a smile and a shrug.

'T'ra then,' Gail said on the doorstep. 'See you tomorrow – or the next day?' She couldn't keep the appeal out of her voice.

'Don't you start fussing too. I said I'd not let you down and I won't. You don't trust anybody do you?'

There didn't seem to be anything else to say and she would have left, but he put restraining hands on her shoulders. 'I couldn't let the chance go by could I? Did Emily say anything useful?'

'Dunno. It might be.' She was very aware of his closeness.

'She meant what she said about you visiting.'

'I know.' His half apology, real concern, disturbing touch, left her without support. If she could have thought of him as an interfering nosy parker and felt anger it would have been easier to manage. Instead, all she could think about was the heat of his hands on her shoulders. The rest was castles in the air.

He leaned on her. 'I'll *be there*, okay? Nothing'll stop me,' shaking her as if to drive home his sincerity, then letting go. 'See you!' He was inside, shutting the door before she could reach and shut the gate.

Milton came back to school the afternoon of the next day.

'Couldn't make it this morning. Had to get me chitty from the doc first.' He said nothing about Jannie and Gail didn't ask.

Breaktime, and they were walking back to Arden House. Heather, Gail and Milton together, flanked by a spreading crowd of others, Craig and Gray among them. Frost from the night before still whitened grass and rhododendron bushes. The bare twigs of overhanging trees were a whiskery lacing against the ice-blue sky. Air, cut-throat sharp. Milton turned up his collar, sinking his chin, one hand thrust into duffle coat pocket, the other grasping a bag of books.

'I've brought the music,' swinging the bag high. 'Just in case!' He laughed pointedly, looking for response, got none and shrugged. 'Oh never mind.'

'What music?' Heather asked.

'For Gail's Floor exercise tape.'

'I didn't know he was making a tape for you?' She turned reproachful eyes on Gail.

'Didn't you?' Gail tried to sound as surprised; frost reaching down into her insides. She wished Milton had been more careful, but knew there was no reason why he should.

'You know I didn't.'

'Oh! Well he is. I couldn't get a recording and he can play the piece.'

'You must have been planning this for ages.'

'I'd thought...planned...well not exactly planned but...'

'She came round last night and asked,' interrupted Milton. 'What's all the mystery?'

Heather said: 'Oh!' then: 'None,' then tartly: 'I suppose she told you my party's on for Saturday at half seven?'

'Everything but the time.' He looked from Heather to Gail and back again.

Gail cringed. Don't let him see, she was thinking, don't let him guess. Hearing Gray Wilkins shout: 'What's about a party? Who's? When? Where's me invite then?' with a relief she would never have thought possible.

'Nobody asked you,' Heather snapped, stalking across the courtyard and up the House steps.

'Yeah? Vee haff vays off making you talk!' Craig yelled, taking the steps at a gallop and pinning her against the closed door.

'Get lost, Flobberguts!' Heather jabbed an elbow, hand clipping him neatly across the chops before she pulled open the door, shutting it behind her with a crash that Gail felt sure must have been heard halfway across the school grounds. The reaction had been overdone. Craig was livid and she wasn't surprised, with everyone looking on. She watched him come back down the steps, the red marks of Heather's fingers across one cheek, his expression thunderstorm. As he passed, he shot them a venomous look.

'What did *we* do?' She glanced at Milton, then beyond him to Gray. She didn't like what she saw.

But Milton was shaking with laughter. 'That'll teach him!'

'You kidding?'

'Bet you. By tonight he'll be boring us all with corny jokes same as ever.'

Gail doubted it. She had seen the expressions on both Craig's face and Gray's, and read the signs. There would be trouble.

14

They got permission to borrow a tape recorder from the music department and to use the main gym, which contained an old upright piano, after school the following day. Gail told Brad at the club that night.

'I'll be there. Four thirty sharp? Should give us at least half an hour. Enough to give it a try. Be warmed-up ready.' His distorted grin came and went. 'No tea. A sandwich course!'

The pun turned out to have a foot in fact.

'I've made up a sandwich pack, Gail,' Pat said, coming into the bedroom Gail shared, after breakfast that morning. Then seeing her expression: 'Marmite, cheese and Ryvita. So don't say I never listen.'

Gail was too surprised to say anything, and silently accepted the paper bag.

'I can't promise to let you off toad-in-the-hole when you do come in,' Pat added. 'But you can always eat less, and there's a grapefruit for your afters.'

Monday was rice pud. Tuesday unfailingly steamed treacle stodge, so she was getting special treatment. She put the packet in her haversack, wondering where the catch was.

Pat lingered. 'You have lost weight you know. It's all the exercise I expect. You've really stuck at it. I must admit I never thought you would...not after packing it in,' retrieving a stray sock and handing it to Gail. 'I'd like to see you in action sometime. Mrs Clapton says you're very good.' Pat aimed a quizzical, faintly despairing look at the back of Gail's head which was lost because she was intent on buckling her haversack.

How does *she* know, Gail was wondering, and then realized it must be through Brad. So he and Hilary talked about her did they? She wasn't sure how she felt about that.

'You should get a kick out of it,' Milton said, helping her to unroll the matting in the gym after school. 'If he bothers to chat about you that means you're of importance to him.'

'Brad never chats.'

'There you are then!'

'But why to *her*?'

'Why not? You're like a police dog sometimes. All sniffs and suspicion.'

'Bitch.' She didn't like the comparison, but it needed to be right.

Milton let out one of his rollicking laughs. 'If I called you that, you'd pull out that sub-zero look of yours and I'd be solid ice!' The mat was level and ready, and he sat down on the piano stool as if grateful for support.

'Do I freeze people?' Gail asked, noticing with a twinge of misgiving how tired he looked. It was asking a lot from someone flattened by flu to do all this.

'The Ice Queen of Broadhayes.'

'God!'

Milton played a few chords, drifting into 'Bethena'.

'I've not warmed-up yet. Give us a chance!' She had changed into her gear immediately the bell rang, and now kept on her track suit, starting to run round the perimeter of the mat.

'No reason why you shouldn't warm-up to music is there? I should think it would help.' He changed to a slow march, made a sudden dash into fast syncopation, winding down like an old gramophone record until the chords came out at a snail's slide.

Gail stopped altogether. 'Hey...you're good! But you

can't expect me to vary my pace like that. I'll be wrecked straight off.'

'Sorry. Will this do?' He played the first section of 'Bethena' at a steady throb, repeating just before the development into the slower passage so that the pace remained even.

'Fine.' He was right. Warming-up to music, *the* music, was relaxing and the repetition getting into her brain made ideas flow.

Splits there...turn...up...jeté leaps there...arabesque...to a stream of tumbling there (but the music would need to be faster)...kneel...roll...

Her body was beginning to glow and she developed the warm-up by running on the spot, knees high, following with a few practice leaps. Then on impulse, twitching into Charleston movements – kicking sideways from the knees, shoulders and hips angled, palms smoothing circles in the air.

Milton looked up from the keyboard and caught her eye. They burst out laughing.

'Not bad. Could be a basis to build on.' Brad came across the gym, nodding to Milton, looking at Gail. 'D'you feel it like that?'

It had been a spontaneous bit of foolery, but now she stopped to think, it did feel right.

'Play it through again will you?' Brad said.

Milton played it through. Once; twice; three times...until they lost count. The Floor exercise slowly began to emerge, Gail shedding her track suit, and by ten past five the first tape recording was made. Rough and unfinished though the routine plan was, Gail felt happier than she had done for months.

'Thanks,' she smiled at Milton warmly.

'Yes, thanks.' By the piano, Brad put out a hand.

Milton shook it gravely, then collected his music.

'I'll have to put my skates on if I'm not to be late,' Gail

122

said, wanting to do anything but that. Her inclination was to stay with him. She felt they were in harmony, as if the music and his willingness to spare time and effort to help her with it had bound them close in a way that had nothing to do with boy–girl friendships; going out. She looked at him with grateful wonder.

'I suppose you wouldn't . . .' Milton began and stopped, changing whatever he had started out to say into: 'That party of Heather's – you *are* going?'

'You say that as if I might have changed my mind. I said yes didn't I!'

'The way you and Heather have been acting lately, I wondered, that's all.'

So the rift had been noticed. Only one day, but it was evidently enough. She wondered if he guessed at the reason and felt cold. If he pinned it down to jealousy of himself, she was sure she would not be able to handle the embarrassment of trying to explain that the situation was not quite as he imagined. She still did not understand it herself. But for the present, the prospect, though unnerving, was lost in a glow of gratitude which she felt to be flowing out of herself and wrapping round them both.

No – not gratitude, she thought, that's too smarmy a word. *Oneness*!

She gave herself a small shake. He'd die laughing if she said that to him. She'd die too, but not laughing.

'Hilary's waiting for us in the car park. She's going to give us a lift, so you can skate at a slower rate,' Brad said.

Hilary again! But even that couldn't spoil her contentment. She asked Milton curiously: 'What was that first thing you were going to ask me?'

He gave her one of his enormous grins. 'I'll tell you at the party!'

Music was already blaring generously when Gail arrived at Heather's house. It was her first visit and she

123

was impressed. As she rang the bell, she wondered if the neighbours had been invited to save complaints. Not that neighbours would be much affected. The house was large, detached, of weathered brick, and standing back from the road in a garden lavishly planted with Cupressus trees. She was surprised by the size of everything.

The door was opened by a young man whom Gail had never seen before, but who could only be Heather's brother. Light from the hall framed the same chunky body, same freckles, same spaniel eyes. Same chatty manner too as he welcomed her.

'You're Gail I know. I'm Marcus. Come in . . . mind that step. Heather said . . .'

She lost what Heather said in a blast of music which escaped from a doorway with a girl in high cowboy boots, leg-hugging cords and white loose shirt. She was an unknown. In fact, from the little Gail could see beyond the half open door into the party room, there seemed to be a majority of unknowns. Her determination not to be one of the first had backfired. She wondered if Milton had bothered to come.

Marcus waved her towards the milling crowd, accepting her coat and taking it upstairs. She was left trying to raise the necessary nerve to go in, and was met on the threshold by Heather.

'Oh I'm glad you made it. I was really afraid something had stopped you.' Her smile was warm, her tone welcoming.

As if she honestly means it, Gail thought with relief and surprise. Lately they had been like a couple of stalking cats. No rowing, just wariness stemming from Heather's bottled jealousy over Milton.

'Milton's here,' Heather said, eyes sparkling, face flushed. 'We've been having a great conversation. About athletics. Did you know he had some sort of cousin who was a Junior International? A sprinter.'

124

'No I didn't'

Heather gave her a friendly push. 'Go on in. I'll get you something and be back in a tick.'

Perhaps it was going to be a good party after all? Feeling better, but still self-conscious, Gail stepped into friendly noisy gloom. The overhead lights were out and red bulbs had been substituted for normal pearl in the four wall fittings. A black marble fireplace sheltered crackling logs behind a brass guard, breaking down some of the darkness, but it was still difficult to see. She had an impression of largeness, old-fashioned furniture pushed against walls, twisting hip-flicking bodies packing the centre. There was a warm fuggy smell of Brut, sausages cooking and joss sticks. Edging through she came up against Cathy Thomas looking like a healthy ghost in a long dress of some pallid see-through material. She was dancing with a telegraph-pole youth, all thin elbows and bent knees.

Cathy swung from him. 'Hi!'

'Seen Milton?' Gail asked loudly to overcome the music blast.

'That the boy with the *fantastic* hairdo?'

Gail shouted: 'Yes,' to Cathy's back, and: 'Where is he?' to her front.

'Over there.' Cathy jerked her head towards the fireplace.

And there he was, sitting on a low sofa against the wall, holding a glass of beer in his hand. Gail had a strong visual impression of shadows pierced by eyeballs and teeth which, for a hairline second, seemed to hang in the air; independent. He got up, seeing her, and she realized that he was dressed in black, shirt and cords. Firelight flickering over his skin produced a sheen. Above, the crown of hair. Fantastic, as Cathy said.

'Found you!' A triumphant voice in her ear, hand on

her shoulder, shattered the vision. Marcus was holding out a waxed paper cup.

She said: 'Oh! Thanks,' and took it, gulping out of nervousness as if it was squash. Her throat scorched; ears were on fire; breath stopped. She coughed like a maniac.

Somebody gripped her arm, took the cup, thumped her back. 'Punch,' Milton said returning the cup but still holding her elbow after the paroxysm finished.

'You don't need to tell me. That's just what it felt like. Whatever's in it?' She wiped her streaming eyes.

'Private recipe!' Marcus winked. 'College special.'

'I've brought you a drink,' Heather said, joining them. 'Some of Marcus's College special.' She saw Milton's hand tucked where it was.

Gail blew out her cheeks, holding up the cup she already had, laughing. 'I don't think...' she saw Heather's smile close down. 'Well thanks all the same. I'll save it for the minute.' She eased from Milton's grasp, took the second cup and set it on the mantelpiece. Of all the luck! Why did Heather have to be so touchy? Breathe in Milton's direction and she turned greener than parsley.

'Want to dance?' Marcus bellowed.

She took the safe way out and nodded, discreetly swallowing the rest of the firewater then joining the throng of gyrating bodies. It was a relief to disappear into music; feel it take over her body, swim with her blood, release the lurking rhythm. Marcus wasn't a bad dancer she noticed, but not in her class. She knew, without being big-headed, that she outshone most in the room. It was just something she could do – thinking with her body as she did in the gym.

The LP came to an end and they paused. Marcus was admiring. 'You're not half bad. But then you are a gymnast so I suppose that's to be expected.'

'Don't always go together.' She liked him. He was friendly. Open. She'd stick with him if she could. Save problems. A faint regret touched her, thinking of Milton.

'Like another snort of College special?' Marcus asked.

'I haven't finished the one Heather brought.' But when she reached for it someone had helped themselves.

'I'll get you another.'

She knew she ought to refuse. Dancing and the first drink on an empty stomach had made her head float. But she didn't want to give the impression of being only a kid who couldn't hold her booze. A devil-may-care mood was taking over. She said: 'Thanks,' drinking it down when he returned, excited and a little scared by the sensation of tingling looseness in arms and legs. Someone put on another record and she danced again with Marcus. With the telegraph pole. Marcus again. Losing touch with time and enjoying herself with a crazy abandon until her head felt like a spinning top.

'Oh!' She flopped on to the sofa by Milton.

He drained his glass, placed it on to the floor then sat back and slid an arm round her. 'You dance great. Look great too. That a new shirt?'

It was. Weeks of scrimping had gone into it – eking out pocket money between gymnastic expenses and the slow-growing shirt savings. The Clothes Book system bypassed because she had been grimly determined to shop where she pleased, buy what she fancied, instead of being nailed down to a couple of stores where the Social Services department had accounts. She looked down with approval at the full jersey top and the way the drawstring gathers flattered her narrow hips – then dizzily up, seeing Heather, like a waitress, juggling with two plates piled with hot sausage rolls.

A warm fuddle of affection for her spread over Gail. Every bit of her body was alive with it. Even my finger-nails like her, she thought, and beamed goodwill – not sure if there was any response, but it didn't matter either way. Swinging her torchlight smile round to include Milton, noticing as she did so how a heat-haze wobble surrounded everything.

'I think,' Milton said getting up, 'you need some grub to mop up the booze.' He grabbed four passing sausage rolls.

'I'm not plastered,' Gail protested, accepting the two he gave her.

'Never said you were.' Milton jammed himself against her. 'Precautions, that's all. Good party.'

Gail nodded, decided it was better not to, and scoffed the two rolls. A smoochy late-night disc was playing, volume turned up. It occurred to her that she hadn't seen Milton dancing at all. She put her mouth against his ear. 'Shall we do this?' Heather was busy. She couldn't mind.

But as they got up she saw Heather, minus plates, coming towards them. Then Milton, wrapping his arms round her, blinkered her with his shirt. Out of sight, Heather became less important. Feeling strangely distanced from her head, Gail thought – anyway she doesn't own him! And gave herself up to the joy of leaning. Even our knees are together, she told herself happily. Nothing mattered but Milton. Milton's heartbeat. Milton's scent, warm sweet spicy...pickling spicy. She began to giggle. Pickled Milton! No...*she* was pickled. Hot as chillies and pickled as an onion. Without him as prop she'd keel over!

As the giggles communicated, Milton bent his head, burrowing between hair and her ear. 'What's so funny?'

But she couldn't tell him and it didn't seem to matter. His mouth wandering across eyebrow, forehead, nose, came down on hers as she lifted her face. She felt a singing shock. A small alarm bell sounded somewhere under layers of woozy excitement. Heather. Heather's party. Everyone looking. Trouble...

Emerging foggily from the kiss she said: 'No.'

'Why not? Ah...go on, Gail!'

'Not here. Everybody's looking.'

'At us?' His snort of laughter blew across her cheek. 'Use your eyes, girl. We're not the only ones.'

But she was still blinkered by shirt and wanted to keep it that way.

'Ostrich like always.'

'What d'you mean?' she protested, hardly caring.

'Bury your head in the sand. Stop yourself from seeing things as they are . . . now don't get uptight,' as she stiffened.

'I'm not!' How could she with him so close? She felt giddy and leaned more heavily. Now was all that mattered, the eyes almost unimportant, and the questions 'What things?' a whisper at the back of her mind. He was slowly but positively guiding her backwards, blind as a mole, she didn't know where until they reached the hall and the sheltering darkness under the staircase.

There was a sudden blast of light as the door to the cupboard under the stairs opened. Marcus's hearty embarrassed voice said:

'Sorree . . . mind moving your feet so I can get at the bucket? Somebody's puked and didn't quite make it to the bog.'

Gail jerked away from Milton, caught her elbow on a broom handle and in trying to catch it, kicked over the bucket which wasn't silent plastic but clattering metal. To her agonized ears the row was enough to bring all the party-goers crowding for a look-see. She finished off by cracking heads with both Marcus and Milton as they all bent down to pick up the bucket. Milton began to laugh. She went hot, almost outraged that he could find anything at all funny. It was her turn to say sorry and as she struggled up again, saw Heather looking over Marcus's shoulder. Their eyes met, the exchange lasting only an instant, but it was enough. Heather turned away.

'Thanks!' Marcus retrieved the bucket. 'Carry on.' He

would have shut the door again, but Gail was already on her way out.

Milton caught hold of her arm. 'Where are you going?' She tugged, wanting only to be free, but he hung on. 'Don't be daft. You heard what he said. They don't care.'

The acute embarrassment which had mixed together with a bitter wish that she could go back to the beginning, knock on Heather's front door and start the party all over again, changed to sick exasperation. Hadn't he seen? Didn't he *understand*? Her head was spinning. Too much trouble to try and explain even if there were words to do so. She said fiercely:

'Let go of me!' scanning the hall. Heather gone. Nobody but the girl in cowboy boots crossing to the stairs. As he released her, Gail made for the front door, not caring where she went so long as it was away from everyone else. But just as she was almost there, someone pounded the knocker and rang the bell simultaneously. She came to an abrupt halt, in her tensed up state over-reacting with a flood of adrenalin as if she had gone round the corner of a street and been suddenly confronted by a lion.

The Stones disc ended, and over party sounds Marcus's voice tumbled from the top of the stairs: 'Answer that someone will you?'

With titanic effort Gail managed the last metre, but while trying to sort out the combined mechanics of yale lock and door knob was shocked again by rhythmic beating of the knocker. Whoever it was must be in an almighty hurry, she thought – opening the door a crack and peering out suspiciously.

'Hi, Cadbury! Anybody at home? Open up. Nobody but a skeleton could get through that titchy space.' Craig Priestley shook his head warningly. 'Now... now...' wedging a thick suede boot between door and door-frame as she tried to slam it shut. Behind him, a dim motley of heads and indistinguishable bodies. Gray Wilkins was the only other recognizable face. She could feel the door pressing against her.

'Not very friendly are we?' Craig said. 'It ain't your party. Not manners to shut out guests.'

'You weren't invited.' She leaned hard, but knew it was a losing battle, forced back, treading on unseen toes. Heather was behind.

'I'm sorry...' Gail shook her head in helpless apology, feeling doubly at fault.

A single puzzled hurt hating look, and she was ignored. Flushed and frowning, Heather glowered at Craig, first in, then at the bunch shoving after him. Five, six, seven? Gail was too bemused to count. They seemed to fill the hall. Hard cases, she thought. A right lot of yahoos.

'You weren't invited.' Without knowing Heather repeated Gail's words. 'You can't come in.'

'We *are* in.' Gray smiled evilly and flicked the end of her nose with finger and thumb.

Already overwrought, volcanic rage stirred in Gail and erupted over them. 'You heard what she said — take yourself and your mob and get the hell out!' lamming down on his raised hand. She was shaking as if she had a high temperature. It was her third mistake.

After split-second surprise, Gray asked quick-fire: 'Who d'you think you are...Crippling Cadbury Champion Coon Wrestler?' the booze on his breath swamping her.

A rattle of laughter. Whistles. Yodels. From a tight bunch the group eased out, fingering pictures on the walls, ringing a brass bell on a shelf, picking up the phone:

'Allo, allo! Dis ees your friendly neighbourhood spy. Come ovfer ant see me sometime...'

Someone behind had grabbed Gail's arm, locking it in a painful grip. Over her shoulder she saw part of a cropped head; to the side, Heather bunched in; in front, Marcus cat-nervous halfway down the stairs and Milton against the newel post at the bottom, looking across heads at her with fury and something else – a wary watching tightly wound caution in his face and body. With a burst of understanding she thought – *he's had to face this before*.

'Who are you?' Marcus asked a shade too loud.

'Guests,' Craig said with cheeky innocence.

'Guests my foot ... leave that!' as a vase of dried grasses rose from beside the telephone high in the air, gripped by pincer hands which slowly opened. There was a tinkling crash of broken glass. Heads began to pop out of doorways and Marcus blustered: 'If you don't push off I'll phone the police.'

'He'll buzz the fuzz!' A ragged falsetto chorus dissolved into cackles of laughter.

'Not much of a mate are you,' Craig said. 'Fancy asking us along then getting nasty!'

A yob with mountain shoulders backed him up. 'That's right. Be more máty. Howsabout a birthday kiss, darlin'?' turning to Heather and holding her in a bear hug, banging down his mouth.

She evaded a direct hit with a swift twist of her head, the kiss landing on her jaw.

They're smashed out of their brains, Gail thought, and saw Marcus rush down the rest of the stairs in a rescue attempt, but be pushed back. A few of the invited males who had been hanging round the door, moved forward, hesitated, moved again with some half-hearted shoving, were shoved back and returned the shoves with more heat.

Someone called out: 'Why don't you push off home?' releasing a flood of insults.

In the middle of all the racket Gail sensed a change and felt a surge of alarm greater than before. She tried to wrench free. A firework of pain exploded in her shoulder joint, running down her arm. She cried out, aware of bodies crushing up around her. Was released. Still unable to get out, she saw Milton's head bob up from a confusion of flailing arms and fists which were to some extent hampered by lack of space, but found enough targets to hurt and stack up the anger. Grunts, squeals, cursing, the scrape and thud of overturned furniture reached her as she elbowed and was elbowed in return, getting nowhere. She looked round desperately for Heather and found her wedged in a corner between door and wall, eyes closed, strong arms circling wildly like a demented windmill.

A frantic hysterical desire to laugh hit Gail. This was crazy! They were all bananas! She'd seen fights at school – usually two doing the scrapping, the rest a circle of onlookers shouting encouragement – but this was more like a boiling stew of bodies. No one directly hammering anyone. Just random punching and lashing out with feet. And where was Milton? Underneath? A heel caught her shin, putting out laughs. Panic grabbed her. She must get out... out... OUT...

But it was no use. Flanked on all sides, whimpering with despair, she saw Milton surface, nose bloody. In front, Gray struggling and butting in the stew, arms caged, shouted something and Craig rising on the stairs behind, taller than Milton now, angled his hand down, felling him like a tree.

Milton pitched sideways, hit his head on the newel post and slumped into the tangled web of arms shoulders necks heads backs, slowly slithering out of sight.

Heather screamed once, like a signal. The fight, as if it had been a soccer game with the final whistle blown, simmered down, parted, drew back as she and Gail, independently and together, pushed to where Milton lay motionless on a scuff of mat. They crouched down, both deaf to surrounding sobs and muttering or the phone being lifted and dialled. Blood from Milton's nostrils ran thickly over the sculptured curve of his mouth and chin.

Heather put out a hand. Didn't touch him. Whispered: 'I can't feel his breath.'

'Christ!' Gray was staring down rigid with horror.

'Christ...' looking up and across at Craig who with
bruised green face had his back against the staircase wall,
'you've killed him!'

15

A cruel finger of sunlight poked at Gail's shut eyes. She pulled the sheet over them for protection. Felt smothered. Pushed it back. Was probed again. Gave up. Sat up unthinking. Groaned at the shoulder stiffness. Then smacked by the memory of the night before, groaned again.

Ambulance, police, Heather's parents (called back from their bridge party), the whole outside world it seemed, had descended, organized, questioned in varying degrees of disapproval. Milton (not dead after all, but more Gail didn't know) had been stowed into an ambulance and carted off to hospital. All that after Gray, Bri and Co. had made a scrambling dash from the house, and before Mr Stafford had driven her back to the Home in frozen silence to spend an agonized night of half-sleep and nightmare wondering if Milton would live and if her aching shoulder spelt wreck for the Individuals and all her dreams.

A memory of Milton very flat, very still on the stretcher with a red blanket to his chin, punched her now, but she was too spent to cry any more. In the night she had hissed all the worst words she could think of into her pillow. Beaten it. Then wept until it was sodden, emerging from this desolation with bloated eyes and the knowledge that like it or not her attachment to Milton was genuine, strong and she was stuck with it. She refused to let the word 'love' enter her mind. She couldn't (daren't) think how Heather would take the attachment. Time would show.

Time did. Later that Sunday morning after she had confronted Pat over the breakfast table.

'You surely aren't going to train this morning?' Pat, teapot in hand, raised plucked eyebrows at her across the children scooping up porridge and crunching toast.

'Got to. Can't miss an Elite group session at this stage.'

'But you look like death.'

Gail thought – thanks very much! Said: 'I'm okay.'

Pat searched delicately for the right words. 'But supposing... um... they want to ask you a few questions? Routine of course – that goes without saying. I'm only thinking of...'

'If you mean the fuzz,' Gail interrupted, 'then you can tell them everything I told you. I didn't miss out anything important. And if that won't do, send 'em to find me. I'm not going to scarper. Now can I have a cup of tea?' Avoiding all the interest shown by the other breakfasters, she glared icily, and Pat, after a single glance, poured the tea in silence.

Forcing down some porridge and taking some toast with her out of duty to Brad's instructions to begin each day with a good meal, Gail left to catch the bus, and found Heather already at the College gym when she arrived. Sick inside, she went and sat down by her on the bench. 'Heard anything?'

Heather was unlacing her training shoes and didn't look up. 'He's conscious. Mum rang the hospital this morning. But he's got to stay put for another night at least.'

'Why? What's wrong with him?'

'Concussed – I think.'

'Why only think? Either you're concussed or you aren't, and it's severe or medium or mild.' She was sharp and aggressive with anxiety. The bad night wiping out any patience.

'How d'you expect me to have all the answers? I don't work there do I? I only know what they told Mum. I'm not a doctor.' Heather, who was just as scratchy, wrenched at the knotted lace. Broke it. Swore.

136

Gail felt a splash of compassion, noticing the catch in Heather's voice and her eyes looking like little sultanas squeezed into flaky pastry. They'd both had a hard night. Heather without the consolation of knowing Milton fancied her. If it was a consolation. She rubbed the creaking shoulder.

'I'm sorry.'

Heather kicked off her shoe. 'Fat lot of good being sorry now. You should've thought about that before. Fat lot of good being mealy mouthed. Carrying on behind my back when I trusted...' She sniffed, fumbled for a handkerchief, failed to find it and rubbed her nose on her sleeve.

'I wasn't...' Gail began and gave up. What was the point? Pierced and truculent and hating herself on both counts, she wished desperately to retrieve their shattered friendship, but knew it was futile. Clocks didn't reverse. She said: 'It just... happened.'

Blood swarmed into Heather's cheeks. She scraped off the other shoe with a toe and flung it away. 'Oh yeah! Tell me another one.'

'No plan. I promise.'

There was a short silence while Heather frowned deeply, Gail's head filled with shock and shame at resorting to weak excuses, and Brad came into the gym.

Heather stood up and for the first time looked directly at her. 'You expect me to believe that?' She didn't wait for an answer but made one parting shot before Brad could reach them. 'Don't think you can win that easy.' She moved away to a mat in the far corner of the gym and began to warm-up.

So it was to be a competition after all.

'You look as if you've lost a quid and found half a p,' Brad said. 'And had a night on the tiles doing it. What's up?'

She told him enough to cover the shoulder injury and watched the grim lines of his face grow grimmer.

'You haven't tried the shoulder out yet?'

'No.'

'Glad to see you've got some sense. Take off your track top.' She obeyed and he felt her shoulder with skilful fingers, moving over her scapula and raising her arm, stopping as she flinched.

'If I'm right and our luck's in, I'd say it's only a muscle wrench. A week for the mending. But we'll not take chances. We'll have another opinion.'

She asked: 'Hospital?' with a great stomach lurch.

'No...not yet. A mate of mine. Bone and muscle wizard. I'll phone and see if he can give us a quick appointment. Meanwhile *rest it*.'

She supported one arm with the other, encouraged only a little by his use of 'us' and 'we': suffering more twinges of anxiety than pain; shivering inside. 'Have I rubbed out my chances?'

'Reduced. You don't need telling what even one week of no training means at this stage. And the injury...'

He didn't need to finish. She said flatly: 'No point in me staying now then.'

He saw the desperation in her face and put a hand briefly on her sound shoulder. 'Wait till Mr Penrose arrives, then I'll go and phone. It isn't the end of the world yet, lass.'

Wasn't it? At that moment she felt that not much could happen to make the day more gruesome, and waited in frostbitten despair, not helped by the sight of the others warming-up.

Old Penrose appeared and Brad vanished. Unable to stand the warm-up activity she went and stood outside the door.

'Five thirty,' Brad said coming back. 'He's broken his No-Sunday-Work rules for you. Star treatment! I'll pick you up at five. Now get off home.'

She didn't go back to the Home. She went to Milton's house and met Emily Box coming out.

'Nobody there I'm afraid, love. Gloria's just gone down to the hospital,' looking at Gail shrewdly. 'Yo were hoping to see Milton?'

'No, just looking for news.'

'Ah! Yo went to the party then?'

Gail said: 'Yes,' warily, expecting caustic remarks about the youth of today, but they didn't happen.

Mrs Box went straight to the point. 'And yo want to know how bad he is?'

'Yes.'

'Well, love, I won't pretend that a knock like he's had coming on top of that nasty dose of flu isn't a bad thing to happen, but he seems to be picking up steadily. When his mum rang the hospital this morning early they said he was comfortable. They'd've said poorly if he wasn't making progress.'

Gail remembered that she had been a nurse and felt reassured. 'That's good . . . oh that's ace!'

'Worried were yo?'

'Scared stiff.' It was like having a haversack of bricks lifted off her shoulders. She had been terrified that he might be dying. 'I got in a panic. Kept thinking the worst.'

'Seems to stop the rest of life don't it when yo have a worry that big.'

'You can say that again!' Gail smiled. The kindliness, the understanding and the simple way her fears had been soothed, cheered her.

Mrs Box smiled back. 'If yo don't mind walking slow, I was just on my way home to make a bite of lunch. Yo're very welcome – or just a cup of coffee if yo'd rather.'

Gail said: 'Coffee please,' and took her arm.

Mrs Box's house was terraced like Milton's, but unlike

139

in that the front door opened straight into the main room. Everywhere was very plain and clean.

'Come through, love.'

They went into the kitchen which was as spruce as everywhere else and surprisingly new with a white sink unit, and a storage heater under the chimney breast.

'Had the old range taken out. Spent too many years blackleading as a girl. No point in courting work, that's my opinion. Save yourself for the things yo really want to do.'

The remark, so common-sense if it had come from a younger person, set Gail wondering if there was anything left this elderly person could possibly want to do? She watched Emily bustle about, boiling the kettle – listening to her chatter.

'Sit down, love. Make yourself at home. It's really nice to have a visitor. I do like company. Never been one for shutting myself up like a hermit. And there's nothing like a young face about the place to cheer things up.'

Gail was surprised. It was more normal to be considered a nuisance.

Emily set the cup in front of her. Daresay yo'll be thinking me a sentimental old fool, but I've always fancied a granddaughter, or a niece would do.' She laughed at herself, pushing the sugar bowl towards her. 'Help yourself.'

'I don't take it thanks.' Gail sipped the coffee to clear a sudden roughness from her throat so she could bring out the name that had stuck in her mind. 'I know you said Bella didn't have any family, but what about her brothers?' thinking – castles in the air need to be got rid of... that's all I'm doing.

'Yo remembered!' Emily sat down, smiling. 'I can say that Jack didn't. There's not much yo can do when you're dead! But Luke... last I heard of him he'd got himself a job carving gravestones. More than that I don't know. I went out to Canada a bit before Bella died, see. We wrote, but after...' she shrugged. 'Now if it was the Admiral yo wanted to hear about, and his Grandad he was so proud of, that would be different.' She drank some of her coffee, silent for a moment as if gathering her recollections. 'A big man with one arm the Admiral was. Come from Bristol. And his Grandad one of them bare knuckle-fighters who'd been a slave. A long time back that was.'

Gail's interest increased. 'We went on a trip to Bristol,' she said. 'They took us to this exhibition about slavery. There was a poster about a bare knuckle-fighter.' She dug back in her memory. 'Midnight they called him.'

Emily was astounded. 'That's him – the very same!'

'There couldn't be two, could there?'

'Not with that name I shouldn't think. Well I never, well I never...' she kept on shaking her head as if she couldn't take in such a coincidence. 'Talking like this brings it all back clear as yesterday. Time's a funny thing. The older yo grow the shorter it gets. Yo've not had enough years to find that out.' She began to laugh again. At herself. 'Hark at Grandma going on!' then wiping her eyes: 'Don't take any notice. Tell me about yourself. Milton says yo're a gymnast. Very good he says.'

Gail let out a heavy sigh. 'I dunno about that. I keep mucking up my chances. Latest thing is I wrenched my arm.'

'How did yo do that?'

Without any effort at all, Gail found herself telling Emily in detail about the party, about gymnastics, about her keenness to do well in the Individual Apparatus Championships, about the possibility growing out of that of being able to compete in the Champion's Cup.

'It's held in the Albert Hall.'

'And yo have to win this Apparatus whatsit?' Emily asked.

'Not win exactly. You don't have to be a medal holder.

Just in the first six.'

'Well I never. And here's me going on eighty-four and not knowing any of this. Only what goes on in the Olympics, and a bit of wrestling. I like to watch that on telly. It's good for a laugh.' Emily flexed an arm. 'Yo wouldn't think now as I used to do weight-lifting.'

Gail's mind flipped. 'In the Olympics?' she asked, astounded.

Emily burst out laughing, shook and wept with laughter. 'Oh dear me . . . ' She wiped her eyes again. 'No, no . . . when I was in training as a Suffragette.'

'Did they send you to prison?' The question sprang out before Gail could catch it, but the old woman didn't seem to mind.

'Yes.'

'That must have been horrible.'

'It was. Don't look so worried. It was a long time ago now. A very long time. And the way I see things, bad or good, nothing's ever wasted.'

'If my shoulder stops me going in for the Individuals, you can't say that's not a waste,' Gail objected.

'Don't meet trouble halfway.' Brown eyes looked into amber, and Gail thought with astonishment – we're talking like people, not an old woman and a teenager. Her shoulder creaked just the same, but she felt better. 'I'll remember,' she said.

'And I'll tell Gloria yo called.' Emily drank the last of her coffee and put down the cup. 'If there's any news of the lad I can telephone.'

'Will you? Oh thanks ever so.' Gail stood up. 'That was nice coffee.'

Emily came with her to the door. 'Don't yo go fretting about your shoulder either. Yo've got four weeks yet. Miracles can happen.' She kissed Gail's cheek.

'It'll take a big one,' Gail said, astonished all over again.

But it didn't need a big miracle. The Bone and Muscle Wizard pronounced it a wrench, nothing worse, did some massage, and recommended ten days rest from training.

'What did I tell you?' Brad said as they left the clinic and climbed into Hilary's waiting car. 'Not a death sentence after all.'

'Ten days though,' Gail moaned. 'That'll leave less than three weeks. *And* I'll be back to square one, having to get fit all over again.'

'You'll make the Centre of Excellence weekend,' Brad said. 'I didn't tell you this morning. Didn't want to raise your hopes before we got the okay. You and Heather have been selected.'

'Me?' Gail couldn't believe it. The Foam Dome gym, the National coach, Lilleshall all tumbled through her brain.

'Yes you. Isn't it splendid.' Hilary's smile shone like her hair.

'When is it?' Gail asked.

'Two weeks.'

And I'll be stiff as a board all over, she thought, plunged into the depths remembering Milton chained to his hospital bed, unable to work on the Floor exercise tape with her. Then dropping deeper and deeper because she ought to be concerned for him alone, useful or not, but was unable to put the gymnastic side out of her mind. She knew she should be elated. Selection for this very special group meant she was earmarked as a top gymnast, even a possible for the National squad if she proved herself. But instead of joy, the fears dragged at her heels. Perhaps her shoulder wouldn't mend quick enough. Perhaps Milton was more ill than they were letting on. Perhaps he'd be in hospital for months. Perhaps . . .

With conscious effort she switched her mind to Heather. The only ray of light. Having been selected together suggested a fresh start. It would still be competition, and they

143

might not be able to be friends any more, but there was a hope they could be honest rivals.

Was she kidding herself? The three-tailed knot with Milton in the middle was tied as tight as ever. Milton in bed in hospital. Everything revolved round Milton.

'You can still use your mind,' Brad said as the car slowed down outside the Home. 'Train it. Think out your routines in detail. Practice channelling your thoughts – remember Malinova!'

She nodded and got out, shutting the door, looking at Brad and Hilary together in the two front seats of the car, thinking – doesn't that woman have a husband of her own? Then raising her good hand as the car drove away.

The phone rang five minutes after supper was over.

'For you,' Pat said. 'Mrs Box.'

Gail ignored the obvious curiosity, going into the Housemother's sitting room and picking up the receiver.

'Hello!'

'That yo, Gail love?'

'Yes.'

'It's about Milton. I saw Gloria and told her yo'd called round. She says they'll be keeping him in for observation a day or two. They don't want to take any chances with him being fresh out of bed. There's always the chance of complications. Better to be safe than sorry.'

'What sort of complications?'

A short pause.

'Are you there?'

'Yes. I was just trying to sort my thoughts. When yo've been a nurse your mind gets clogged with medical terms. It's no good me spouting a lot of stuff that'll mean nothing. Take it from me that a good rest is the best thing for him.'

'Did he...was there any message?' Gail asked awkwardly.

'Not that I know of love. Gloria didn't say.'

She felt upset and realized that she had wanted very badly to know that the party hadn't spoiled things between them. But she was being stupid. He was ill, or anyway not well enough to bother with messages.

'Are yo still there, love?'

'Yes I'm here.'

'D'yo want me to give Gloria a message to take from yo. She will, I know.'

'You can say I hope he gets well soon, that's all.'

'Right yo are, love. Good-bye.'

'Thanks for ringing – bye.' Gail put down the receiver and Pat came into the room with an alacrity which meant she had been standing in the hall hoping to pick up conversational crumbs.

'Everything all right?' She smiled tentatively. 'I don't know this Mrs Box do I?'

'I dunno. She's nobody special. Just the friend of a friend.' Gail didn't want conversation, longing to get away on her own, but Pat said:

'There's something I've been wanting to talk to you about, Gail. Sit down, dear.'

Reluctantly she perched on the edge of a chair with an air of bored resignation.

'I've been thinking about you having to share a bedroom all the time. You've a lot on your plate at the moment. Mrs Clapton says...'

'What does she want to go poking her nose in for?' Gail interrupted, the disappointment and anxiety over Milton breaking up her bored act and coming out in unreasonable irritation.

'That's unfair,' Pat began tightly...then sighed and allowed a small self-mocking laugh to escape. 'The situation is this. David Price will be leaving at the end of the week. His mother has come out of hospital. So the single room will be free. Would you like it?'

145

Gail had been caught out by her own ill temper and knew it. The offer was marvellous. She knew that too and said: 'Yes,' and 'Thanks,' with a pause between, because it wasn't possible to say good-bye instantly to the scratchiness and be smiling and grateful as she knew she should.

'Right,' Pat said. 'He's going on Saturday, so you can move your things in on Sunday.' She nodded dismissal in a way suggesting she was still ruffled.

At the door Gail hesitated. 'If you like you could come down with me to the club one night... when you aren't on duty.' She was off-hand. 'That's if you still want to see us training.'

'Oh yes I would!' Pat's response was immediate and sincere. Gail caught a hint of surprise in her expression. She found she could smile now.

'Okay,' she said, and left the room, going upstairs.

16

November edged into December, became frosted and pearly with razor-sharp air and breath in clouds outdoors. Indoors, Gail, shoulder almost as good as new, worked valiantly to regain lost ground. Milton came out of hospital, and meeting for the first time there had been constraint, but it had gradually eased. He hadn't referred to the party and neither had she, drifting back into friendliness; never officially 'going out' (he never asked her) but together sufficiently to make it more than ordinary friendship. Hurt at first, she decided in the end that this new relationship suited her much better because it was undemanding and fitted in with the training – in particular their work on the tape. They spent hours on it together with Brad, polishing and re-polishing, aiming for perfection. Milton had abundant patience, playing 'Bethena' a hundred times or more, altering pace, watching Gail so he could blend the music with her movements. Note perfect now. Apparently tireless. But it was two weeks before he returned to school.

'What's the rush?' he said when Gail questioned him. 'I'm having a ball. Tinkling the ivories or feet on the table! And our Emily trotting in to make me cups of coffee. Who needs school?' They had laughed together, but she still felt concern.

The Centre of Excellence weekend came and went. Gail, approaching it with nerves wound to breaking point, emerged on the other side elated, full of awe, drowning in despair. The work had been exacting and though her shoulder had survived under Brad's supervision, she felt she hadn't done him or herself justice. Heather had been much more composed. Much more in command of her body.

'Relax. Let your muscles stretch out...amplitude, remember?' Brad said more than once. 'You're defeating yourself with anxiety, lass.'

She had tried, but so much seemed at stake. The Apparatus Championships only ten days off, her explosion into front rank gymnastics seemed fragile and precarious to a degree that she couldn't believe the luck would hold. Sharing a student bedroom at the college with Heather hadn't helped in the relaxing process. They had been presented with this arrangement. No choice. A knotty situation which Gail had tried hard to smooth out by chatting. Heather answering only with unusual brevity.

'He's ace that's why,' when Gail spoke of her surprise at learning that Brad was now a permanent coach at the Centre of Excellence.

'I know that, but it's so quick. He's only been around since September.'

'August.'

'All right, August. No time.' Really she was relating her own return.

Heather shrugged. The conversation died. They got into bed in silence and Gail lay for a long time staring up at the ceiling, remembering Lilleshall, the confidences, her secret joy in finding a friend and being admitted into that friend's most private yearnings. Only a few weeks and so much had happened, so much had gone wrong, so little right. Then everything had seemed, if not simple, at least clear. Gymnastics came first. Who-am-I a close second. Enclosing both, the warming bonus of a friend. Milton no more than an uneasy shadow between them. But since that humiliating party everything had fallen apart. She no longer felt sure of anything. In her gloomier moments doubting even Milton and Brad. She had never wanted to be involved in anyone. She was a loose straw blowing about. All that guff about the Bristol Knights...

A laugh and sob combined in her throat and she bit her lip to keep both down. Loneliness opened up like a crater and she fell in, to be enveloped in the worst attack of blown-up fears she had experienced for months, which grew more and more fierce until even the ceiling she was staring at seemed alive with threat – lit by a sudden eye of light (in fact thrown from car headlamps) which observed her with cold malevolence.

She sweated. Reached bottom. And because there was nowhere else to go, began to inch up, finding on the way one positive fact. She clung to it like a drowning rat to a floating log. The Individuals ahead, a barrier between her and the Champion's Cup. She had to get through. If it meant training until she dropped and then getting up and training some more she must do it. *She must succeed!*

There was a cloying smell of sweet talc, anti-perspirant and disinfectant in the changing room. Gail, washing her hands, was acutely aware of this and a hot tension winding round her own inner tension. After all the waiting, thinking, training, tears, fears, despair, anticipation, the Individuals had arrived. She was here. In Cardiff. Compulsory routines completed yesterday. About to compete in the Voluntaries today. She shivered.

Several other girls adjusting leotards and track suits, putting on ballet tights or taking them off, combing hair, tying ribbons, finding handguards, gym slippers, hairgrips, were also obviously keyed up. Revealed in sudden giggles, high-pitched chatter, off-hand shrugs. But more than that the very air seemed to have an electric charge.

Like static, Gail thought, drying her hands and half expecting sparks to generate. She was conscious of having seen one or two of the competitors before, even knew some names. The bouncing Meryl was there; Stella and Judy

149

also from Lilleshall. But most were unfamiliar. She would have liked it better if they had all been strangers – except Heather. This adventure with the drive down, both of them with Brad in Hilary's car, had drawn them together. Not friends, rivals still, but in an area where they were as equal as any two separate gymnasts could be. The thought produced a lift of satisfaction as she checked hair for tidiness, then equipment – keeping to the order which brought good luck. And as a final touch to the luck, took off the little silver St Christopher Milton had given her as a mascot, making sure it was safe in her training bag. The small warm pressure spot it had made against her breastbone stayed for a moment. A comfort.

'You ready?' Heather asked.

'Almost.' Closing her eyes briefly, she calmed her breathing, mind murmuring the instant jingle. Opening them again to find Heather staring at her with curiosity, but all she said was:

'Mum and Dad got here at last. They had an awful journey without the car. Nearly missed the connection.'

Gail felt a very small twinge of envy. To have support. People who cared. Watching. Rooting for you . . .

Then they were in the corridor and she saw Brad. Solid, grim, dependable. *There*. Envy dwindled, died and was buried under the bustle and sorting of people into groups as they lined up preparatory to filing into the gymnasium. Noise from the audience seeped out through the doors. Sweet sound. Terrifying! She exchanged a look with Heather. No need for words to understand they shared the same apprehension, the same fizz of adrenalin. A momentary panic hit Gail. All yesterday she had felt like a novice. Today was no different, and yet this was a National championship. She would be competing against the cream of British gymnasts. It was a joke that she was here. A big laugh. The luck couldn't last. Today she'd fall apart; muff that high bar backward straddle; her shoulder would give out on the Tsukahara vault; she'd break her neck...

> Malinova Comaneci Korbut and Kim
> Malinova Comaneci...

A hand on her shoulder. On Heather's shoulder. Brad linking them. The half-light of the corridor pulling strange shadows from his scar as he smiled. 'You've done well enough up to now, so don't forget me lasses, you're as good as the best!'

The chatter, movement, people, resolved into order, quietening to an expectant hush as the doors swung open and taped music suddenly blared.

Gail saw Brad nod, then make a brief mime. A last reminder to position her grip accurately on the asymmetrics and keep the distance right. Recently she had made one or two slips. She nodded and began as the others began, to walk spring-heeled into the gymnasium and gathering applause.

Four elements. Four groupings, and Gail found herself waiting to vault. She scanned the gym. Not to learn the positioning of the apparatus – all was familiar after the Compulsories – but to slip on the feel of the place like a comfortable overcoat which could then be forgotten.

Judges at tables angled to achieve the best view for each piece of apparatus had notepads and forms laid out. Small runners, smart in their club colours, crouched ready to sprint with messages and scores to the overall judge at the main table, where a microphone stood amongst the papers. The judges assessing the vault sat side on to the horse. Several vaults had been performed. The girl in front was preparing herself – waiting for the controlling judge to raise his hand. Time to blot out everything but the length of blue matting which led to the Reuther board and horse beyond. Gail measured the distance. Printing it into her mind. Focusing on the spots where her hands must smack down. Feeling muscles and tendons become alert as the girl went over, rose up with a quick spreading of hands above head before walking away.

A short pause while judges recorded the marks.

Now it was to begin. Now!

Instinctively Gail licked the tips of her fingers and ran them lightly down her thighs, watching for the signal.

Now!

Elevated. Poised for a fraction of time on her toes. And she began to run, gaining speed and power as she went. Bursting with a release of energy, yet controlling it. Pacing right. Hitting the Reuther board right. Flattening the first body flight, with a half turn and thrusting down strongly as she tipped over. Knowing instantly that her hands weren't perfectly placed as she kicked savagely towards the horse, stretching her body to maximum. Into a pike. Stretching out again – this time to land. But under-rotating and falling forwards on to hands and knees.

Disgusted, she went back for the second attempt. Glowering at the floor. Acutely conscious of Brad's bland expression as he said: 'Kick back even more strongly at the horse.' It was a bad start. The marks would be low. Seven point nine five . . . oh God! Shades of Lilleshall!

She had observed Heather's vault. Not quite so loose as her own, but not perfect either. The mark – eight point three five. As she waited for the senior judge to signal the second attempt, resolution burned inside her with white heat. Concentrate . . . concentrate . . . Just her and the apparatus. Nothing and nobody else.

The signal came. She licked the tips of her fingers, touched her thighs and was running, bounding, flying, propelled by an explosion of energy that was all the while under her control. As she went into the tight pike, turning in the air, she was conscious of a difference – it was good . . . everything had come together – and landed, steadying herself with only a short step forward.

Beam next, and Heather performing with grace, pulling off a testing cartwheel dismount with elegant assurance.

Gail murmured: 'Professional!' as Heather, breathing hard and suppressing a smile of satisfaction, passed her. The smile flowered. Only an instant, but something in the expression reached out. Was it respect? There was no time for reflection now. Gail looked at the polished beam of wood. Strong. Narrow. A four inch width on which to dance, tumble, balance. She focused on it. Obliterated everything but it and herself in relation. Looked for the judge's signal and with a diagonal run, took off from her outside leg, scissoring the inner forward and up, hand supporting. From the moment she landed in a squat on the narrow path her bones told her everything was right – would be right. She stood up, confidence spreading through her limbs. All she had to do was focus. Think with her body. Listen to it.

'That wasn't bad. Good as you've done in a long time. Got the mark you deserved.' Brad patted her back. 'Shoulder okay?'

Praise indeed and she glowed, nodding. 'I haven't finished yet.'

'No.'

'A lot can happen.'

'Yes. Good if you focus on what you have to do. Bad if you talk yourself down.'

She listened. He was talking sense like always, but could she follow the advice? Self-doubt would sneak in.

'You've got what it takes...lots of bottle. Remember that.'

High praise. She went to the asymmetric bars and flew. But Heather flew as well. Spurred on by whatever Brad had said to her, or just because the day was right and she was right? Gail didn't know, watching the other competitors and the mounting marks. Adding hers in her head, but not retaining enough of the overall scores to

153

know exactly where she stood in the table. She knew she was doing well, but was it well enough? Observing a thistledown girl spin over the upper bar — airy bird-swift — with respect, even awe. Did she perform like this? Were her line, shape, planes of body, movements as flowing and graceful?

And then the group, finishing, was ready to move on to the last exercise, but there was some marking problem for one of the beam competitors. A long wait followed while marks were checked, papers exchanged, judges murmured together, and Gail felt the hard-conquered tension return and begin to tighten. A terrible restlessness seized her. Oh to pace about! Run. But all she could do was bend and stretch, flex such muscles as she could on the spot. She thought of Milton and hummed the first bars of 'Bethena'.

'They're taking long enough,' Meryl said in Gail's ear.

'What's gone wrong?'

The massive shoulders shrugged. 'Marks don't match up I expect. Someone scoring too high and someone else not giving enough.' She seemed very knowledgeable.

'Whatever . . . I wish they'd get their fingers out,' Heather murmured, drawn in. She let out a short anxious snigger, looking to Gail as if for support. 'How's your score?'

'So so. Twenty-six to now. That's . . .' Gail used her fingers to add up: 'fifty-nine point seven counting the Compulsories as well. And yours?'

'Twenty-five ninety-five . . . sixty point one altogether.'

Was there a note of triumph? Point four in front, but no way of knowing where that placed them. For entrance to the Champion's Cup she must be in the first six. Again Gail murmured the magic names in her jingle — Malinova Comaneci Korbut Kim — observing each Floor exercise until it was time.

'Good luck!' Heather whispered and almost broke the

carefully built walls of concentration with this piece of generosity.

Gail stood alone in the centre of the floor-mat. Waiting. It was very solitary there. The eyes of the world on her. She knew as the thought came that it was rubbish, but couldn't rid herself of it until she caught Brad's eye. His attention, total absorption, was directed towards her. The power and force she had so often sensed, came out to meet her; prop her. She was no longer alone and felt grateful. Then resistant. This was no time for relying on props. She should be alone. She was *herself* when she was alone. The things she possessed, her body working for her, mind making it work, thoughts, skin bone heart blood – this was what she was. *Who* she was. And all as it should be.

The judge raised his hand. She heard the familiar chord. Pictured briefly Milton's hands on the keyboard, strong black against ivory. Simultaneously her body assumed the pose so often practised, working into the introduction and first stream of tumbling. Nothing existed but music and muscles obeying, not flawlessly, but well. She knew she used the full extent of the Floor area, going from corner to corner, not overstepping its edge; felt her tumbling to be fluent, leaps high, timing precise. Hesitating with only a brief loss of balance in one complex twist and roll. Finishing with a flourish and keeping her upswept arms, arched back, weight curving one leg, for the full dramatic seconds needed to bring the exercise to a polished conclusion.

'Nine point one five,' Brad said putting his arm round her shoulders as they stood back against the wall. 'Satisfied?'

She shook her head. 'I'm never satisfied.'

He looked at her quizzically: 'Not until...?' leaving 'Olympic Gold' unsaid.

'Not even then.' She heard him laugh, but couldn't think of anything except her score of today – thirty-five

155

point one five. The waiting was a torment and the judges seemed bent on dawdling – comparing papers, shuffling papers, rearranging papers.

She shut her eyes, trying to still the shiver which kept attacking.

'Ladies and gentlemen...' The microphone crackled and yowled.

Gail's eyelids which had flipped open, shut again as the microphone was adjusted, tested, adjusted again, tested again.

'Ladies and gentlemen. Sorry to keep you waiting. Technical troubles.' The announcer had a blocked nasal voice. 'I'm not the only one with a cold it seems!'

Laughter.

Gail felt almost bursting with impatience. The effort of keeping herself from yelling out was like corking a volcano.

'Well now, you are all waiting with baited breath I am sure to learn who is the overall winner of the competition. With a splendid total of seventy-three point two marks it is Judith...'

Gail felt her heart slither into her slippered feet. Seventy-three point two! She did not dare look at Heather. Listening as Gold, Silver, Bronze medals were awarded for Vault, Asymmetric Bars, Beam...

'And with a total of eighteen point seven for her Beam exercises, the Bronze to Heather Stafford.'

Gail joined in the applause, glad and despairing, warm and frostbitten. All that was left was the Floor. Had she a hope there? No. Impossible. Loss of balance, the last twist and roll messed up.

All medals were awarded. The thistledown girl winning Gold again for her Floor exercise, having already walked off with the Asymmetric Gold. Gail was not among the winners. A great feeling of desolation stole over her watching the medals presented with handshakes and kisses. She had failed. Worse still, she had failed Brad.

'And now, ladies and gentlemen...' the microphone boomed and screeched bringing yet another prolonged pause with the announcer raising his eyebrows in despair. But finally it behaved. 'Ladies and gentlemen, in case you haven't managed to keep a check on all the marks, I will run through them now...'

Gail listened attentively but without hope. Fifth... Sixth...

'Sixth is the competitor who won a Bronze medal for her work on the Beam – Heather Stafford.'

Despair was absolute, yet under it a respect for Heather's achievement. Gail struggled for composure, clapping hard.

The announcer held up his hand for quiet. 'I should tell you ladies and gentlemen, that this sixth position was almost a tie – one tenth of a mark between the overall scores of Heather and her team mate from Coventry's Leofric Gymnastic club, Gail Knight. A very creditable performance, Gail. I think she deserves our congratulations. Better luck next time!' He began to clap, the applause swelling as the audience joined in.

The awful despair didn't vanish, but it faded. The gloom and sense of failure lifted a little. Gail felt cheered. Then disbelieving. Then the despair came back but not quite as strong. Panic touched her because she hadn't reached the coveted sixth place. Was it always going to be like this? Trying and trying with nothing but failure?

Brad tapped her on the shoulder. 'Move yourself. Line up. They're waiting.' He was pointing at the Press photographers positioning themselves to get the best shots.

Head buzzing, hardly aware of her feet taking her back, she joined the others in the arena. Two pictures of her were taken. Once with all the competitors. Then she and

Heather alone as fellow club mates. She blinked with each flash of the bulb.

'I'll look terrible!' she said to Heather when it was over and the audience and competitors had reshuffled into eager gossiping groups slowly moving towards the doors. The Staffords and Hilary were with them. Brad in the background was talking to one of the organizers.

Hilary smiled. 'You were splendid. And Heather... a Bronze... marvellous!'

'You danced on that beam like it was six feet wide instead of four inches, Heather love.' Mrs Stafford was almost in tears. 'Both of you a grand pair. We'll have to celebrate...'

'Ginger beer strictly,' Mr Stafford said and everyone laughed.

Gail, still swimmy in the head, became aware of a touch on her arm. She looked down. A small girl in red trousers and sweater, crinkly hair tied in white ribbon bunches, light polishing her ebony skin, was looking up with wide inquiring eyes. She pushed a paper and pencil at Gail.

'Please... your autograph please?'

'Fame at last,' said Heather, noticing.

Astonished, Gail signed and handing back the paper asked on impulse: 'D'you want to be a gymnast?'

'Oh yes!' The eyes were full of longing.

They shared shy smiles.

The incident, so small, made a big impression on Gail. For some reason she couldn't explain, she was moved almost to tears. She gave herself a shake. You've been overdoing it, she told herself, you're knackered that's all. But the happening had happened. The little kid stuck in the forefront of her mind until Brad and Hilary sprang the final surprise of the day. Even then the kid was there, hovering in her red trews and new sweater. Smiling. Admiring.

They showered and changed into ordinary clothes,

then went for a meal, afterwards parting company. Heather was travelling back by train with her parents. Gail and Brad climbed into Hilary's car. When they were settled, Brad said:

'Here ... a reward for you. Something you've been after for a long time.'

Hilary turned in the driving seat, smiling. A slip of folded paper in her hand. She held it out.

'I didn't give this to you before because ... well you had enough to think about.'

Gail took the paper and opened it, glancing down. A photocopy of a birth certificate. Hers! She read through column by column.

When and where born: Nineteenth October 1964: 56 Broadway, Coventry.
Name if any: Gail
Sex: Girl
Name and surname of father: [here a blank]
Name, surname and maiden surname of mother: Audrey Knight
Occupation of father: [another blank]
Signature, description and residence of informant: A. Knight
                                        Mother
                                        56 Broadway
                                        Coventry.

When registered: Twenty-first October 1964
Name entered after registration: [cancelling ink stroke]

She read it through several times, trying to understand the implications, but her brain seemed to have changed to cottonwool. Hilary had switched on the engine and Brad had his back firmly turned. In the back of her mind Gail was grateful. As they moved out into the traffic she was scarcely aware of the passing streets. Cold facts going round in her mind. Name if any – Gail. Name, surname and maiden surname of mother – Audrey Knight ... nothing else. Audrey Knight. Audrey Knight.

Audrey Knight. Nothing about her father. It didn't seem strange. She had never thought much about any father. Audrey Knight. Her *mother's* name. But that was all it was – a name. No body. No voice. She couldn't see or feel anything. It was the name of a stranger, that was all. It didn't tell her anything.

The car halted at traffic lights, and reflected in the driving mirror Gail saw Hilary's eyes looking at her. 'Does it help?'

There was no straight answer, only a jumble of unsorted feelings and vague hints at some meaning she couldn't yet grasp. A new way of looking at herself which had tendrils winding back into this momentous day. She said the only thing she could:

'Maybe.'

The lights were still red. They exchanged another look. Hilary, on the verge of saying something else, hesitated.

'What?' Gail asked.

The lights chose that moment to turn amber then green and the answer didn't come for some time. When it did, it only added to her confusion.

'The address doesn't exist.'

'But I know the road. It's near Heather's house.'

'The road, yes. The number, no.' Driving mirror eyes briefly expressed concern. 'I'm sorry.'

Brad twisted so that he could look round at her, hooking an arm over the back of the seat. 'That sequence of yours on the beam – backward walkover into handstand then to half circle turn...' His voice battled against her enveloping thoughts. Almost against her will she was dragged back into the present. 'Are you taking it in?' He gave her a quizzical look.

She made a final spurt into the present, leaving the past behind. 'What was that about my forward roll?' this time concentrating as he described again where she had gone wrong, and his ideas on how to improve the sequence by expanding part of a particular movement. The effort of imagining how it would work didn't allow for brooding. When he had finished she thought – cunning old devil! But perhaps he wasn't cunning? Perhaps all he was bothered about was her work and how to raise the level of her performance, the rest didn't matter. Whichever it was, she realized that he had succeeded even if by accident.

She went back to looking through the window, fingers absently playing with the St Christopher on its chain round her neck, thinking over the new move, getting it fixed, connecting it with the rest of the sequence. Feeling the whole in the marrow of her bones.

17

Brad was talking to Mrs Capucelli just inside the gym. He looked round as the door opened.

'Gail...I've got something for you.' He felt in the pocket of his track top and held out an envelope.

'For me?' She was amazed. Nobody ever wrote to her. She couldn't remember the last time she had received a letter.

'Miss Gail Knight it says. See?' He handed it to her.

A narrow pale mauve envelope. She took it. The writing was small and looped but very neat. Completely unfamiliar. The address was 'c/o The Leofric Gymnastic Club, Coventry'. The postmark was London. She turned it over gingerly. There was nothing on the back but a smear of ink.

'Came to Mr Penrose first,' Brad said. 'When you're ready I'd like to have a quick word about your beam dismount before you start warming-up. I've had thoughts about it. Improving thoughts. Perhaps using a Rudolph ...you know, front somersault with one and a half twists...' He nodded and left her.

She felt extremely relieved that Brad had been postman. Penrose would have stood over her, breathed down her neck, probably wanted to know who had sent it, might even have asked what was in it! She didn't want curiosity from him or anyone, and to avoid it tucked the letter in her pocket and retreated to the toilets. Inside the cubicle with the door shut, she felt more secure and took out the envelope, slitting the top. There were four sheets of thin mauve paper folded in quarters. No address and no date. She read:

Dear Gail,

I saw a photo of you in the Western Mail after you had been in Cardiff and read about you belonging to the Leofric Gymnastics Club in Coventry. It gave me quite a turn and I have not known what to do for several days. You see it could be that I am writing to the wrong person which does worry me but not as much as letting this chance of writing slip by. I *have* to write. Things have been bottled up for so long but I would not want to upset you and hope you understand this. I suppose if I was sensible I would let sleeping dogs lie. But I am not always sensible which is why I am taking this risk of writing to you now though feel sure it is *not* a risk. Even after all these years and with it being only a newspaper photo which are never very clear there was *no mistake*. I would have known your face anywhere. You look just like your dad...

Gail felt suddenly weak and sat down on the lavatory pan. The writing seemed to dance on the page and she had to blink hard before it came back into focus. With an effort she read on:

He was a lovely man and good-looking and I loved him very much. When he was killed in a motorbike crash the world seemed to end for me. He was mad about motorbikes which is why he came from London to Coventry to work in the Meriden factory. I worked there too in the office but it was having the same name that first drew us together. It seems queer to me now when I think about it that I am living in London and he is nothing but ashes scattered about the cemetery garden in Coventry.

Perhaps I shouldn't be telling you all this but it has been locked up inside me all these years. Believe me I did not wish to abandon you. But what could I do with Stan dead and no one to turn to? You see my parents were very strict religious people. I cannot tell you how strict they were. You would need to live in the house that I lived in as a girl to understand. They did not hold with dancing or going to the pictures or being taken out by boyfriends and it was two visits to the chapel on Sundays. If they had learned that their only daughter was in the family way without a wedding ring on her finger and no hope of one it would have killed them. But that is all water under the bridge now. They have both passed on and I am married after all. My husband is a good man but does not know anything of all this and I must keep it that way.

God knows (and I mean that quite respectful) I would give all I have to start all over. Believe me I never wanted to leave you. *Believe me*. I wrapped you up nice and warm and left you at the Welfare for safety. It was all I could do.

There isn't much else I can tell you about your dad except he was an only child same as me. His dad had been some kind of artist a sculptor I believe though he carved gravestones for a living. He died before I met Stan. He never spoke of his mum. It is not much for you to know but I think it only right that you should. I would not want you to think that your mother is quite heartless. *Believe me* not a day has passed since you were born that I have not thought about you.

The newspaper says you may take part in a competition at the Albert Hall on the 20th of January. It is not often I can be away from home for long but if things permit I will try and wait outside the morning before the competition, hoping for a sight of you though I would not be able to stay long.

> Yours very sincerely
> Audrey Jones (née Knight)

Gail put her head in her hands. She was shaking. She could not think. She felt as if a bomb had exploded in her head and fragments of her shattered brain were swirling about. Helpless. Uncoordinated. For a long time she sat there and still nothing made sense. Then out of the chaos one coherent thought emerged. How crazy it was after all the thinking and wondering and hunting about that it should be gymnastics which had dug up a mother for her!

After a while she realized that she ought to get back to the gym or Brad might send someone to look for her. She was not ready for that. She stood up and a second thought hit her. Perhaps the letter was not from her mother at all, but just some raving nutter? She leaned against the wall fighting for control. It would be hard, very hard, to train now, but she must try. How long had she been here? Ten minutes...half an hour? She had no idea. It felt more like a week.

She came out of the cubicle and splashed cold water over her face thankful that no one was there, and did some deep careful controlled breathing. It didn't help her thoughts, but her body felt better. Then scraping together all her courage, she went back into the gym and apologized to Brad for taking such a long time.

'Is everything all right?' he asked.

'Yes.'

'You don't look too good.'

'I ... I felt a bit faint that's all. It came on just before coming here tonight, but I'm fine now.' She tried to smile.

He gave her a long shrewd look, but seemed to accept this. 'Right. Now...we've a lot to go over. First I want to tell you that you've been picked as reserve for the Champion's Cup.'

She felt a swell of excitement. It had been on the cards, she had guessed that, but there was a vast difference between guessing and knowing.

'Pleased?' he asked.

She nodded, feeling the excitement cool a little. It was only *reserve*. What did a *reserve* do except sit and watch?

'The end of January may seem weeks away, but it's no time at all if you are to be at the top of your form.'

'For reserve?' The semi-question was petty she knew.

'Don't be daft!' He frowned at her. 'A reserve needs to be just as fit and prepared as those competing. What use is an unfit unrehearsed gymnast? Might as well not bother to turn up. Let's have less of the self pity and a bit more work...a lot more work. In the gym and at home. That bedroom to yourself has improved your training facilities. You need somewhere for private thought. Somewhere quiet to get yourself sorted.' He put a hand on each of her shoulders. 'Never underestimate yourself. It's as bad as

165

being big-headed...worse. Whatever your label you're a gymnast first...right? You're going to a top gymnastic event...right? If you're to be at a peak then you've got to work till you drop...right? Every reserve needs to be *ready*. It *matters*...right?'

She nodded, stirred once again by his energy, and surprised once again by this knack he had of getting through to her. He really cares, she thought. The way I perform matters. *I* matter. She was still shaken rigid by the letter, but not so bad. And she was reserve. *The* reserve. She was in!

'Get warmed-up,' Brad said, letting go of her and patting her back.

18

Boxing Day brought snow and a party at Milton's house.

'Jannie's birthday, see,' Milton said when he asked Gail
to join in. 'Good enough excuse to ask everybody!' and he
burst into one of his irresistable laughs.

He hadn't exaggerated. When Gail arrived, the whole
world seemed to be there. Friends, neighbours, old, young,
in-between. Everyone except Heather. She had been
asked, Gail knew, but had turned down the invitation
because it was Boxing Day and she had been given
another invitation to another party. Surprisingly she
hadn't seemed upset. As things were, it hadn't been
possible to ask for reasons, but Gail felt obscurely relieved.

She stood looking at the door spattered with wind-
blown snow. Hung on the Grecian urn was a ring of flowers made from scarlet green and silver foil tied with tinsel
and frosted with more snow. But knocking wasn't necessary. The door opened and Milton came out to meet her,
snowflakes patterning his hair and crimson shirt. He put
an arm round her shoulders, kissing her lightly.

'Saw you coming up the street.'

Gail was taken by surprise. He hadn't kissed her since
Heather's party. It was disturbing, but excitingly so, and
she found she didn't mind. The house was full of good-
humoured laughter and noise, with talk and music boom-
ing out, and the sweet smells of baking, coffee, beer,
wrapping round the constant flow of people in and out of
doors, all of them open – and dancing too she discovered
when, in search of Jannie, Milton took her into the back
room where furniture had been cleared to make space. She

was caught up in the easy friendliness; made a part. She could not feel an outsider.

They found Jannie in the kitchen with a small friend nicking fresh baked casava biscuits, and Gail delivered the necklace present she'd brought, then followed Milton into the front room, where a table groaned under a weight of pies, cakes, sandwiches, fruit; cans of beer beneath; bottles on a side table. Mum Gloria was there. And Milton's dad – a stout man with Milton's eyes and laugh. Emily Box was there too, sitting on the sofa, mince pie in one hand and a glass of beer in the other.. She raised the glass to Gail.

'Come and join me, love. I want to hear more about your doings before I lose yo to the dancing. Milton tells me yo've been picked for a special team for the gymnastics.'

Gail took the coke laced with a splash of rum from Milton, and sat beside her. 'I'm only reserve.' She could say it cheerfully now. In spite of Brad's encouragement in the gym she had dived into a steep-sided gorge of depression the next day. Hauled out by Brad yet again, caustic and unyielding as ever.

'You're proving that the way things went couldn't have been any different.'

'What d'you mean?' She had been stung. Tears rising.

'Anyone who can't take a setback on the chin without flinching isn't tough enough for this game. I thought you'd got guts. Else I wouldn't have given you the time of day.'

'Why did you then . . . go on tell me, why did you?' She had blazed at him, tears almost turned to steam by fury at the seeming injustice coming on top of this blight to her hopes. For the first time in her experience she saw him hesitate, and set her jaw, glaring at him, truculent, poker-backed, whole pose unconsciously made arrogant by anger.

When he smiled she couldn't believe it. He ran fingers

through the iron grey stubble of hair, raising it to hedgehog spikes.

'You aren't the only one with ambition. I have it too. If I could've gone out there into an Olympic gym and tried for a Gold myself I'd've done it. But I'm not put together right. I haven't got what you may have ... "may" because you've got to show it's there. You're built right, intelligent, *and* you've lots of bottle. I've got the last two but not the first. But I'm a bloody good coach. Even so, without gymnasts I'm nothing. Just as without a coach you're nothing. We need each other. And I'm ambitious for you and myself together.' Smiling still, he had slapped her across the thigh. Painfully hard. 'Now get back and show what you can do.'

She had gone to the asymmetrics, seething, determined to show him she wasn't defeated, that she was steel not putty.

When she finished he said: 'Excellent.'

Never before had she heard him give anyone higher praise than 'Not bad'. She shone with satisfaction and pleasure. The glow lasting the rest of the day, trailing into the next, and never quite dying. It was with her now, helping her to talk freely with Emily.

'Now get a chance to be part of the show.' Emily was sympathetic. 'I call that a real shame.'

'But I'll *be* there,' Gail said. 'I'll be in the audience, front row, see everything.' She took a large steadying sip of rum and coke to bolster her spirits which threatened to slip. 'It'll be good experience.'

'When is it? And where did yo say?'

'End of January at the Albert Hall.'

'Ah ... London!' Emily said with obvious relish. 'Now I remember, yo mentioned it before. I wouldn't mind a trip there to watch yo. See the old haunts.'

'You can have a free ticket if you like.' The idea of having a friend to take was suddenly very tempting. 'I get two.'

169

Emily looked startled. She was just saying it, Gail thought, enthusiasm pin-pricked – she didn't mean a word. But Emily, after a swig of beer, grinned, her expression more like a girl than an old woman.

'Why not! It's about time these old bones got stirred. Make the most of life, that's what I say. Never turn up a good opportunity. Gets yo into trouble sometimes, but it's worth every minute.'

Milton came and perched on the sofa arm, glass in hand, asking: 'What is?'

'Grabbing opportunities even if they get you into trouble,' Gail said.

'I'm all for *that*.' He winked. A definite deliberate wink.

She said firmly: 'We were talking about the Champion's Cup. I'm giving Mrs Box one of my free tickets.'

'Emily – now we know each other better,' Emily said. 'I never could abide formalities.'

'What about me then?' Milton took another can of beer, opened it and refilled his glass. 'Don't I get a free ticket?'

She was only allowed the two but didn't hesitate, thrilled: 'Oh yes.' For a split second she wondered how to lay her hands on this third ticket. The one she was saving would probably never be used, but she couldn't give up the secret hope. The familiar sick feeling that had plagued her since reading the letter came again. She refused to let it get a hold. Heather had her two parents. Now she would have two good friends to be with. She fought to smile.

Milton waved his glass of beer. 'That's fixed then.'

'What's fixed?' His mother came squeezing her resplendent pink silky bulk between a couple standing back to back.

'Tickets for the Champion's Cup, Mum. You know – I told you.'

'London?' She sounded doubtful.

'I shan't be on me own so you needn't fret. Gail's going

and Emily. Anyway I'll be a hundred per cent by then. You worry too much.'

'A real outing!' She was all smiles again, pushing a plate of cake under Gail's nose. Rich yellow cake stuffed with raisins and cherries. 'Try a piece of cornpone, love. Baked it myself.'

Gail took a slice, then a second. The diet could go hang tonight, she thought. It was a very small rebellion but she got a kick out of it.

'Drink up,' Milton said. 'Then we can dance.'

Gail drank up, said: 'See you!' to Emily, meaning it because she was such a game old girl, then wedged herself against Milton and into the crush, swaying and shuffling to the music which boomed round the room, filling her ears and shutting out unwanted thoughts.

Milton flipped the St Christopher on the Woolworth's chain she had bought especially.

'I wear him always,' she said. 'Mascot.'

'He's not brought you much luck.'

'You don't know that. You can't say so. I've lots of times coming yet.' She was unintentionally fierce, goaded by thoughts of the near failure.

'Maybe.'

She had to pull back to see his face, which was serious, not teasing. 'Why only maybe? I *have*.'

'Keep your shirt on. I only meant because nobody knows what'll happen tomorrow or in a week, or even five minutes away.'

'I do. I'll need to get a drink of water. I'm drying up with the heat.'

He laughed then and pushed her towards the door and kitchen, meeting Errol on the way back. Milton introduced them. Errol, plump like his parents, said: 'Water?' in mock horror, laughing like Milton. They chatted for a while, then went back to the sitting room and piled into the food, Gail drinking more rum and coke, Milton sticking to his beer. Emily was still tucked into a corner of the sofa.

'Have another beer,' Milton said, seeing her glass was empty.

'I oughtn't. I'll be kippered.'

'Go on. Never miss an opportunity.'

'Mind yo don't cut yourself, yo're that sharp,' Emily said. 'Yo'll have me under the table.'

'You're on,' Milton said, and they all laughed.

Gail sat by her, feeling relaxed and happy, and when the talk turned to Bella again, found herself asking questions about the family as if they were Emily's relatives, nothing more.

Singing had spread round the room and Milton was coaxed into fetching his guitar. For a while he accompanied, then was cajoled into singing songs composed by himself. Plaintive songs, sung in his light edgy voice, and full of a silvery sadness that pulled tears into Gail's eyes, so that she sat looking at her feet, too embarrassed to wipe them away in case she was noticed, not daring to move in case they spilled. When she had them under control she discovered that there was no need to be so bothered. Plenty of other people were wiping their eyes.

Milton strummed a loud cheerful chord. 'What's this then... a Wake? Come on now... altogether,' drawing them into 'Gimme crack corn'.

Afterwards he went to put away his guitar. Gail had another coke with rum splash and a ham roll to keep her sober. Aware that Milton was taking his time in coming back. She had another ham roll. When he still didn't return, she went to look for him amongst the dancers, then in the kitchen. He wasn't in either place. Rum giving her courage, she ventured upstairs, opening two doors before she found him. He was stretched out on his bed, eyes shut, but opened them as she closed the door.

'Sorry I woke you.' She couldn't help feeling a little hurt because he had gone off without a word.

'It's okay. I was awake. Just tired.'

He did look exhausted.

'Are you okay? D'you want me to fetch your mum?'

'You kidding? She'd go bananas! Sit down. I'm okay.'

She sat on the edge of the bed, not convinced, and he rolled over on to his back, taking her hand 'You're really nice.'

'You too.' She waited expectantly.

He went on holding her hand, nothing more.

She felt awkward; irritation growing. 'What are you thinking about?'

'Hundreds of things.' He suddenly pulled himself up, letting go of her hand and swinging his legs over the edge of the bed so they were side by side. 'Enjoying yourself are you? Mum's an ace cook isn't she?'

Gail ignored the red herring. 'People don't usually go away and lie down at parties without a word unless they feel groggy.' She knew she wasn't being very fair, but the irritation persisted.

'Ostrich one minute, mule the next. You'll be able to earn your bread as a one person zoo!'

'You always make stupid jokes.'

'What's wrong with having a laugh? Better than crying.'

Irritation boiled up and over. 'Nothing's wrong with it – except the timing.' The party which had begun so well was taking a wrong turn. She could feel herself getting more and more uptight. Milton would probably go on cracking more wet jokes. She couldn't stand the feeling that he was shutting her out ... then felt annoyed all over again for allowing herself to be provoked. Deep down was the knowledge that the letter was the key. Ever since it had arrived she'd been touchy. She armed herself against more teasing.

It didn't happen. Instead he sighed and rubbed his

head. 'I'm sorry. It's just that every now and again I get this feeling if I don't lie down I'll fall down, and I don't let on because of the fuss...you wouldn't believe! Flu and a bash on the head aren't the best ways of keeping fit. I'll get over it though.'

Her irritation subsided. Being fit was suddenly a most precious gift, though she had worked hard for it. A gift she possessed. And something which helped her body which she also possessed. Both treasures. She had never thought of good health or her own body as being special until now. Milton had helped her discover these things. He'd helped her in so many ways. She looked at him sheepishly, wanting to repay him, on the point of telling him about the letter, but unable to bring out the words. Still wanting to make amends, she said:

'It's me that should say sorry... being snappy over nothing. I've got this thing about being shut out. Makes me uptight over nothing. I suppose it's because no one wanted me. Parents and that. But I'm learning to get over it.'

He didn't say anything, but hugged her. It was better than any words.

After a while she said: 'Won't they be missing us? Hadn't we better go down?'

'I suppose so.' He seemed reluctant, shaking his head.

'What?'

'D'you really want to know?'

'I asked didn't I?'

'Just thinking about all the times I've imagined you up here with me, and now you are here, well...' His disconsolate look said the rest.

She smiled at her knees. 'There'll be other times.'

He brightened immediately. 'You mean that? Oh *good*!' sounding so enthusiastic that they both burst out laughing together.

19

So this was the Royal Albert Hall! Coming up a wide
flight of steps from Prince Consort Road in the company
of Heather and Brad, Gail felt a burst of excitement out of
all proportion to her role for the day. During the night she
had slept badly in the student hostel where they had
stayed. Pursued by restless striving dreams which kept
rousing her, leaving behind a misty sense of loss that still
hung round even when she was fully awake.

Until now.

She stared up at the immense dome rising against an ice
blue sky pencilled with fine cloud lines. A jet plane cruis-
ing at an angle to the clouds left a crossing vapour trail.
Nearer, pigeons came in a flutter to argue ownership of
some breadcrumbs with sparrows already there – the
quarrel being settled by an old woman in ancient string-
tied overcoat and moth-eaten fur hat, scattering peanuts.

The excitement expanded. The London buildings – sol-
emn Victorian brick, new glass towers – traffic roaring;
bustle of people; underground tunnels filled with the echo
of busking guitars and warm draughts; sudden quiet
squares; these steps; this dome...she loved it all. She
couldn't wait to get inside this great iced cake of a hall.
See it. Smell it. Experience every last detail. For the morning at least she would be part of the action. Warm up and
Photocall – every reserve had the right to those, Brad had
told her.

Before that she had to pass the meeting place. She was
scared and the ecstatic feeling faded almost as quickly as it
had come. Apprehension mounting almost to terror as

175

they crossed the street. She did not know what she would do if anyone was waiting.

A man stood by one entrance to the Hall. Several people were walking along the pavement. No one else. Relief and disappointment rolled together. They went through the black double doors and hung about in the foyer while Brad produced their proof of identity at the Security Check. Then on through more doors to a curved corridor.

'Goes all the way round,' Heather said. She had once been to a concert here. 'Layers of corridors one on top of the other. You'll see the ways in. I expect the changing rooms'll be down below.'

She was right. They were tucked under what Gail later realized were tiers of audience seats. The usual tiled boxes with mirrors and washbasins in arched alcoves, showers and lavatories beyond. Several girls were already there. Gail knew all the faces now, all the names, but hung back, not wanting to join in the chatter. Heather immediately struck up a conversation with Gold-medal Judith about TV coverage, the merits of handguards or no handguards, the best shampoo for dandruff cure, plus a mass of other trivia which drove Gail into deeper silence and made her long to escape. Already in leotard and track suit, she changed quickly into gym slippers, slithering out into the corridor and round to the first entrance she could find.

A flight of brass railed steps led her to the auditorium. She stood perfectly still at the top, absorbing first impressions, hit by the vastness of the place. Tier upon tier of plush seats climbing up to piled boxes, ornate with columns and extravagant gilt. The roof hung with dark mushroom shapes. To her right was the stage, and opposite, the main doors where later the gymnasts, men and women, would make their entrance. She looked down into the arena. It was surprisingly small – packed out now with apparatus already bolted into place, an upright piano crammed against the barrier, a couple of TV cameras

176

being wheeled into position by men in sweat shirts and basketball boots. The place hummed with random organized activity. People with lists, Biros and expressions bordering on desperation. People in track suits, jeans, lounge suits. Uniformed people – a solitary Life Guard in dazzling scarlet and gold. Electricians, radio engineers, cameramen... and down below some gymnasts and coaches. In particular Brad and the National coach she had met at Lilleshall, talking together by the rings.

'Feel me shake.' Heather had come up behind unheard and put her hand on Gail's arm. It was clammy and trembling. 'I hate these beginnings. It's okay when we get started. I feel as if I've got half a dozen prawns swimming in sour milk inside me.'

Gail didn't offer any comment. At this moment she would have welcomed the prawns in their sour milk. Heather didn't seem to notice the silence, burbling on:

'Mum and Dad said they'd try and get here early... wish me good luck. They're bringing Alan with them.'

'Alan?'

'My cousin. Didn't I mention him before?'

You know you didn't, Gail thought.

'He's over here for a sort of working holiday from Australia.'

Gail wasn't taken in by the off-hand casualness. A faint pink colourwash had painted Heather's neck and cheeks. Gail felt slightly shaken, remembering the sea of tears at Lilleshall.

'He's an ace swimmer,' Heather said. 'He's won all sorts of medals and cups. What a body! You should see him in swimming gear... shoulders like sides of beef, tree trunk thighs... oh listen to me twittering on like a loony. It's nerves. But you understand don't you? Known me long enough. I'm a right scrumball getting the dithers like this and talking out of the back of my eyes. I'll be all right now.'

The last remark would have meant nothing if it hadn't been accompanied by the look – open with a hint of self-mockery.

'You can't win 'em all,' she added, and went down into the arena.

Gail's initial reaction to the Australian cousin did a flic-flac, leaving her bewildered. Had Heather been offering an olive branch, hinting she was no longer in competition for Milton? But she could have been genuine. Perhaps the Australian cousin *had* swept her off her feet? Or was it a final shutting down of the barriers with a faked cover-up? Gail shrugged away the problem. Whichever, now was not the time for bothering. Now was *her* morning. Her chance to warm-up and take part. Anything else, even the letter, could wait.

She saw Brad beckon, and began to descend the steps.

The photocall came early. Gail, waiting with the others, couldn't help thinking of the last time, at the Individuals. Flashlights, photographers angling for the best shots, the grouping and regrouping of gymnasts were so similar. If anything was different it was herself. She felt changed. How, she wasn't sure. She knew she felt nervous, with an inner tension which only faded when the Photocall ended and the warm-up began, returning again when Brad warned her that time was getting short and this would be her final Beam practice. She didn't allow her concentration to flicker, working through to the last sequence of walkover to back flip into a twisting somersault dismount with scarcely a loss of balance; the landing perfect.

He clapped quietly, then checked his watch. 'Lunch isn't far off. I want you to have plenty of time to wind down and be ready for the grub. You need to be able to digest quietly.' He nodded at Gail.

'Is there enough time to... to get a breath of fresh air?'

She crossed her fingers, willing him not to ask any awkward questions.

He frowned slightly, re-checking his watch. 'There's a few minutes I suppose, but they don't like gymnasts wandering about. No more do I. What's wrong?'

'Nothing!' Careful. She had said that too quickly. She must be more casual. 'It's all the ... oh *everything*,' indicating hall, people, Press, officials. 'I only want a few minutes on my own, that's all. Just to get my head straight.'

He repressed a smile. 'All right, but don't stray too far. I don't want to be a one man search party. Here,' he held out a card, 'you'd better take this. You need it to get back in.'

Trousers already on, she pulled her track top over her head and pocketing the card, climbed up then down into the corridor. In front of the double doors she paused. She couldn't get rid of the feeling that she was confronting some great barrier. All she had to do was put out her hand and push, then walk outside. It was easy.

She went on standing there, her mind going back over the day to escape having to face what might be on the other side of the door. The morning had been wonderful but agonizing. She knew she had performed well in practice. It was as though her body, perversely, had reached a peak and couldn't do anything wrong. She felt twice as alive. The frustration therefore being twice as acute. If it hadn't been for the other thing, these present moments of solitude would be welcome. A time to prepare for the aggravation of having to be a spectator. She had a sudden intense wish that Milton and Emily were here so that they could laugh and chat lightly about everyday things. But it was too early for them to have arrived. And if they were here, she wondered, would she be able to turn back from these doors and go on with her life without ever facing the woman who claimed to be her mother. *Never find out*?

179

There was no choice.

Quickly, before her courage could fail, she pulled open the door and went out into the sharp air, scanning up and down the pavement, up and down the street, up and down the pavement again.

A thin pale woman with a newspaper stood near the wall. Two men on the kerb were deep in conversation, and a little further on, a Chinese girl very smartly dressed stood holding a bunch of rosebuds. The girl seemed to be waiting for someone. An elderly man being taken for a walk by a dalmatian came between them, distracting Gail's eye away from the girl back to the woman with a newspaper. The woman looked at her. Gail took in the old young face, worn waxy skin, long nose, wide thin mouth, wisps of hair fuzzing the green headscarf, rounded shoulders under brown-belted mac, calf-length fur-topped boots. The woman was watching.

Gail's heart began to hammer relentlessly, as if she had run a mile. She waited. The woman neither came towards her, nor stopped observing, and she felt herself tremble. On impulse she turned away, walking hurriedly round to the front of the building. Stopping for a while when she got to the main entrance to give herself time to calm down. Then, on the way back, made herself walk in a slow casual manner, as if she was just passing the time.

The woman was still there. Still watching. Gail's eyes slid away. Slid back. Surely this stick of white candle-grease wasn't her mother? In spite of the cold she began to sweat. The woman continued to stare. Gail thought – I can't *stand* this – forcing herself forwards; pushing out the question:

'Mrs Jones?'

'Pardon?'

'Er . . . are you Mrs Jones?'

'No, I'm afraid not.' A deep voice. A pleasant smile. A lift of thin eyebrows.

180

Gail muttered: 'Sorry,' backing away, almost knocking into someone directly behind.

'Excuse me.'

She swung round and was confronted by a brown oval face framed in a fur collar, hair tied up in a scarlet kerchief.

'Could you tell me if this is the competitors' entrance?'

Overhead a cloud of pigeons swirled round and down. The sun came out and spread shadows across the street, across the woman, across Gail. She licked round her parched mouth. Tried out her voice. 'Were you . . . looking for someone?'

'Yes.'

'Me?'

'I'm not sure.' The woman smiled shyly. 'If your name is Bernice then I am.'

A hard cold desperation filled the inside of Gail's body and pressed against her ribs. She felt almost punch-drunk – beaten by wild hope, thumped by cruel tricks of fate, sick with disappointment and terror.

The woman eyed her with a slightly puzzled wariness. 'It must sound silly me not knowing, but I've never met Bernice.' She laughed in an embarrassed way. 'A cousin of a friend and she doesn't know London, so . . .'

But Gail could not hear. Only one thing mattered. To escape. She shook her head violently, and turning away blundered back into the building.

Brad came through into the foyer and saw Gail leaning against the doors.

He started to say: 'Where the hell have you been?' because vital time was slipping away and everyone else was going up to the restaurant, but never finished the sentence. She had her eyes shut and was shivering.

'Gail?' He went up to her and put an arm round her shoulders, feeling her stiffen. 'What's up, lass?'

181

She opened her eyes and looked at him mutely, still shivering.

'Are you ill?' He felt sick himself at this possibility.

She shook her head. Still trembling. Still dumb.

Recognizing shock, he debated whether to take her straight to the emergency sick room or to the changing room, and discarded both. The first because it could suggest to her that she was really ill; the second because of all the curiosity and well-meaning damnfool questions. Instead he steered her towards the refreshment room, sat her at a table and bought her and himself tea, lacing both cups well with sugar.

'Drink this.'

She shook her head. 'I . . . can't.'

'Drink it. Take your time. You don't have to gulp.'

Obediently she lifted the cup, spilling some tea because her hand was shaking so much, but managed to take a sip. And when that went down took another. He let her go on sipping for a few moments without bothering her with questions, sitting on his own impatience. When the cup was half empty he said:

'Your friends are here. I've had a word. Said you'd see them at the interval as you wouldn't have time beforehand.' He waited for her reaction.

The meaning took a moment to sink in. 'I know I've to sit with you, but isn't there time to see them now?' Her voice came out husky and tremulous, but the worst of her bodily shaking was over.

He thought – if I was a religious man, now is the time I'd put up a prayer.

He said: 'No there isn't. Can you take another shock?'

She brought her gaze up from the table to his eyes slowly, as if still at a distance, put down her cup, folded her hands and waited.

'Judith Wilson's damaged her knee. It wasn't long after you'd gone. She was all steamed up, not looking where she

182

was going, and went a purler down the stairs on her way to the changing rooms.' He leaned across the table covering her hands with one large palm. 'So you see, the reserve *is* needed.'

There was a long silence between them. Then she said: 'My life . . . is all . . . accidents.'

'It happens. I know that. But you can only make the best of what turns up – or go under, and you've got too much guts for that. You've got to go forward. There's never any brass in looking back over your shoulder. Take life by the ears and if it fights you, fight back. But I don't really need to tell you that. I've seen you battling and winning for weeks now. You've got personality, lass, and courage, and that's what counts.'

Again his dynamic inner strength seemed to pulse from him in great waves, pushing away her numbness and fear and confusion. Another person would have messed around trying to winkle out what had just taken place, but he never wasted time or energy on blind alleys. She could trust him because life had been tough with him too. Always he went straight to the heart. *He understands me*, she thought. It was as if the sun had burst through thunderclouds.

'Well?' He was still clasping her hands, looking at her questioningly.

What was it Emily had said: 'Never turn up a good opportunity.' If this wasn't the most golden opportunity, nothing was. She still felt shaken, but she was herself, alive, and nothing was going to get in her way.

'How much time have I got to get ready?' she asked.

'No time at all. Not before lunch,' he said. There was a look of respect in his eyes. 'You'll be needing some fuel.'

'But I can't eat!' She was appalled.

'You can do anything you set your mind to if it's important enough. *Anything*!'

'But eat?' she pleaded.

183

'You don't have to have a blow out, but you do have to be there. And you will need *some* calories y'know. It's going to be a hard afternoon.'

She took a deep breath, trying to win mastery over herself.

He watched her, feeling absolute sympathy but showing none. 'Are you quite sure you feel up to it?' he asked.

She met his eyes.

'Try and stop me!' she said.

The closed doors were in front. On the other side the band of the Life Guards was rounding off a selection from 'The Pirates of Penzance', the music flowing over the buzz of the audience. In two lines – men and women – the gymnasts waited.

'Any minute,' Heather breathed in Gail's ear.

She didn't answer, eyes fixed on the doors. The music ended. Applause swept out. An amplified voice boomed: 'Ladies and Gentlemen ... the Gymnasts!' and through the open doors she saw scarlet and gold uniforms, raised trumpets, heard the fanfare call. The old things fell away and in that instant she knew that now was all that mattered. She thought, this is ME – what I can do ... this is what I am! And walked forward down the spotlight.